Henry's arms tightened around her. "Are you saying you can't resist me?"

"That's just wishful thinking on your part." Jess longed to brush her cheek against the soft hair on his chest, but she knew she'd be lost once she did. She kept her gaze on Henry's face. He looked determined to get his own way. He was, no doubt, used to getting everything he wanted.

"Jess." He ran his hand along the curve of her waist. "I touch you and something happens to both of us." He paused, his dark gaze on her face. "I get hard. You melt. I can feel you softening under my hand."

She shook her head. "I'm not up for a one-night stand."

Henry frowned. "Who said anything about one night?"

FAMILY

1. **HOUSEBOUND—** *Anne Stuart*
2. **MOONLIGHT AND LACE—** *Linda Turner*
3. **MOTHER KNOWS BEST—** *Barbara Bretton*
4. **THE BABY BARGAIN—** *Dallas Schulze*
5. **A FINE ARRANGEMENT—** *Helen R. Myers*
6. **WHERE THERE'S A WILL—** *Day Leclaire*
7. **BEYOND SUMMER—** *Karen Young*
8. **MOTHER FOR HIRE—** *Marie Ferrarella*
9. **OBSESSION—** *Lisa Jackson*
10. **TRUST A HERO—** *Muriel Jensen*
11. **GAUNTLET RUN—** *Joan Elliott Pickart*
12. **WEDNESDAY'S CHILD—** *Leigh Michaels*
13. **FREE SPIRITS—** *Linda Randall Wisdom*
14. **CUPID CONNECTION—** *Leandra Logan*
15. **SLOW LARKIN'S REVENGE—** *Christine Rimmer*
16. **UNHEAVENLY ANGEL—** *Annette Broadrick*
17. **THE LIGHTS OF HOME—** *Marilyn Pappano*
18. **JOEY'S FATHER—** *Elizabeth August*
19. **CHANGE OF LIFE—** *Judith Arnold*
20. **BOUND FOR BLISS—** *Kristine Rolofson*
21. **IN FROM THE RAIN—** *Gina Wilkins*
22. **LOVE ME AGAIN—** *Ann Major*
23. **ON THE WHISPERING WIND—** *Nikki Benjamin*
24. **A PERFECT PAIR—** *Karen Toller Whittenburg*
25. **THE MARINER'S BRIDE—** *Bronwyn Williams*
26. **NO WALLS BETWEEN US—** *Naomi Horton*
27. **STRINGS—** *Muriel Jensen*
28. **BLINDMAN'S BLUFF—** *Lass Small*
29. **ANOTHER CHANCE AT HEAVEN—** *Elda Minger*
30. **JOURNEY'S END—** *Bobby Hutchinson*
31. **TANGLED WEB—** *Cathy Gillen Thacker*
32. **DOUBLE TROUBLE—** *Barbara Boswell*
33. **GOOD TIME MAN—** *Emilie Richards*
34. **DONE TO PERFECTION—** *Stella Bagwell*
35. **POWDER RIVER REUNION—** *Myrna Temte*
36. **A CORNER OF HEAVEN—** *Theresa Michaels*
37. **TOGETHER AGAIN—** *Ruth Jean Dale*
38. **PRINCE OF DELIGHTS—** *Renee Roszel*
39. **'TIL THERE WAS YOU—** *Kathleen Eagle*
40. **OUT ON A LIMB—** *Victoria Pade*
41. **SHILOH'S PROMISE—** *BJ James*
42. **A SEASON FOR HOMECOMING—** *Laurie Paige*
43. **THE FLAMING—** *Pat Tracy*
44. **DREAM CHASERS—** *Anne McAllister*
45. **ALL THAT GLITTERS—** *Kristine Rolofson*
46. **SUGAR HILL—** *Beverly Barton*
47. **FANTASY MAN—** *Paula Detmer Riggs*
48. **KEEPING CHRISTMAS—** *Marisa Carroll*
49. **JUST LIKE OLD TIMES—** *Jennifer Greene*
50. **A WARRIOR'S HEART—** *Margaret Moore*

FAMILY

Kristine
ROLOFSON

Bound for Bliss

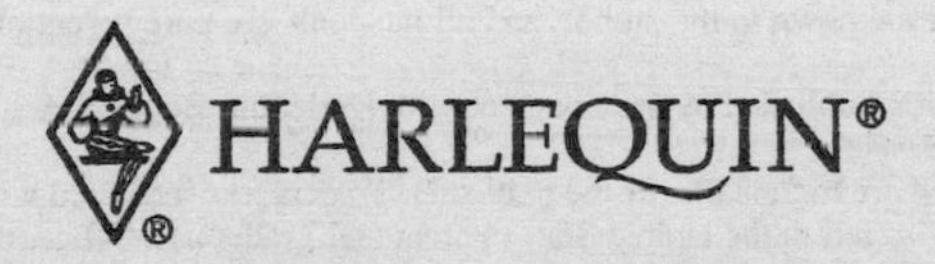

TORONTO • NEW YORK • LONDON
AMSTERDAM • PARIS • SYDNEY • HAMBURG
STOCKHOLM • ATHENS • TOKYO • MILAN • MADRID
PRAGUE • WARSAW • BUDAPEST • AUCKLAND

If you purchased this book without a cover you should be aware that this book is stolen property. It was reported as "unsold and destroyed" to the publisher, and neither the author nor the publisher has received any payment for this "stripped book."

HARLEQUIN BOOKS
225 Duncan Mill Road, Don Mills,
Ontario, Canada M3B 3K9

ISBN 0-373-82168-9

BOUND FOR BLISS

Copyright © 1990 by Kristine Rolofson

All rights reserved. Except for use in any review, the reproduction or utilization of this work in whole or in part in any form by any electronic, mechanical or other means, now known or hereafter invented, including xerography, photocopying and recording, or in any information storage or retrieval system, is forbidden without the written permission of the publisher, Harlequin Enterprises Limited, 225 Duncan Mill Road, Don Mills, Ontario, Canada M3B 3K9.

All characters in this book have no existence outside the imagination of the author and have no relation whatsoever to anyone bearing the same name or names. They are not even distantly inspired by any individual known or unknown to the author, and all incidents are pure invention.

This edition published by arrangement with Harlequin Books S.A.

® and TM are trademarks of the publisher. Trademarks indicated with ® are registered in the United States Patent and Trademark Office, the Canadian Trade Marks Office and in other countries.

Visit us at www.romance.net

Printed in U.S.A.

Dear Reader,

Sometimes doing the right thing can break your heart. In June of 1987 my husband and I, along with our three children and a rented truck, left our home in north Idaho to head east. Back to Rhode Island. Back to family. Oh, we were doing the right thing, we knew. Our children needed a good education and grandparents. We needed a bank account. I needed to write books instead of hanging wallpaper.

So when it came time to write my third novel for Harlequin, I didn't stray far from my own experience of traveling across country in a twenty-two-year-old station wagon with two children arguing in the back seat. You might think you're reading fiction, but there really was a heat wave in Montana, I drove with ice cubes on my head, melted crayons and stinky hermit crabs. My six-year-old tried to shave her legs. The car broke down in Missoula, the parakeet almost died in Wyoming and my son has never visited Nebraska without getting an ear infection.

Oh, yes. We were doing the right thing. Eleven years later I can say that and know it was true, though that summer in 1987 I thought I'd never stop crying. And Jess, my heroine in this story, is facing the same kind of heartache. Adventures are never easy, and neither is love. But broken hearts heal and adventures have a way of turning into funny stories to share with friends. I hope you enjoy mine.

Kristine Rolofson

Kristine Rolofson
P.O. Box 323
Peace Dale, RI 02883

Don't miss any of our special offers. Write to us at the following address for information on our newest releases.

Harlequin Reader Service
U.S.: 3010 Walden Ave., P.O. Box 1325, Buffalo, NY 14269
Canadian: P.O. Box 609, Fort Erie, Ont. L2A 5X3

1

"WHO IS SHE?" Henry Myles glared at the stubborn old man seated behind an ancient oak desk and waited for an answer.

The old man sighed. It was an artificial sigh, Henry knew, designed to make the listener aware he was upsetting a poor, frail senior citizen. G.H. liked to use guilt as a weapon whenever possible.

"It's just a simple request, boy." He reached for his unlit cigar and rolled it between his thumb and index finger. "Don't know what you're making such a fuss over."

"I can't take time off from the marina project right now."

G.H. nodded toward his grandson's arm. "Don't know what good you'll be around here. You can't drive, you can't even hold a pencil, and everyone in Seattle with any sense is taking the summer off. Besides, anybody foolish enough to fall off his own boat..." He shrugged.

"I told you—it was an accident." Henry looked down at the plaster cast that covered his right arm from the elbow to the knuckles of his swollen fingers. The damn thing was too tight, and his arm hadn't stopped aching since he walked out of the hospital emergency room yesterday. Now his head began to throb in time with his wrist. All he wanted to do was walk down the hall to his office, open a window and fall asleep on his new Italian-leather couch. He knew he could count on Martha to hold his calls and take care of business in her typically haphazard fashion until he felt well enough to continue through the day.

"There are no such things as accidents, son," G.H. growled. "You've been pushing too hard for too long." He set the unlit cigar into an immaculate glass ashtray. "You have seven weeks of vacation on the books. You have to take four weeks by October or you'll lose 'em."

Henry looked past his grandfather's bald head to the comforting view of Puget Sound. A large white ferry crawled through the rainy mist toward the Seattle waterfront. "I had planned to spend August sailing around the San Juan Islands," he said, then did a rapid calculation. Today was the sixth of July, and the doctor had estimated that the cast could come off in four to six weeks. He still had a shot at it.

"By yourself, I suppose." G.H.'s tone was almost accusatory.

Henry tore his gaze away from the window and looked at his grandfather. He shrugged and immediately wished he hadn't when the ache accelerated. "That's the way I like it," he said through gritted teeth.

"This month will be sick leave, then. And you'll still have August to do whatever it is you do on that boat."

"Never mind that, G.H. Who the hell is the woman this time?"

"A friend," he said. "That's all."

Henry ran his fingers through his dark hair and counted to ten. "That last 'friend' you told me about cost the family a small fortune to pay off."

"Muriel." G.H. sighed. "She only loved me for my money, but when you're my age..." He frowned at his grandson and his voice sharpened. "A man needs a woman, son."

"I suppose this one's a blonde, too."

G.H. cackled. "Yep." He shoved a piece of paper

across the desk. "Here's her name and the phone number of the restaurant in Idaho where she works. She's a sweet little thing, so be nice."

"Damn it, G.H.! This is one of the stupidest things you've ever asked me to do." Henry eased his broken arm into the comforting fold of a white sling. "I don't want any part of it."

"I've always loved you, Henry. I don't ask for much."

Henry heard the pathetic quiver in the old man's voice, a finely tuned pathetic quiver. He stood up and looked down at the man behind the desk. "How can you keep a straight face when you're trying to con me?" he demanded.

"It's not easy," G.H. said with a chuckle. "C'mon, boy. Do this and I'll never ask you for anything again as long as I live." He inched the piece of paper closer to the edge of the desk.

Henry hesitated, suffering a twinge of conscience. G.H. looked seventy and acted eighteen, but he was eighty-two years old. Henry loved and respected him more than any other person in his life. He picked up the paper and shoved it into his pants pocket. "I'll think about it, but I'm not promising anything."

"You have two days," the old man said. He swiveled in his chair toward the window, but not before Henry saw the satisfied gleam in his eyes.

"GUESS THIS IS the place." Refusing his brother's offer of help, Henry struggled to climb awkwardly out of Peter's red Porsche. The summer afternoon heat surrounded him as he took his bag, his lightweight jacket and the latest issue of *Newsweek* from the back seat of the car and set them carefully on the gravel driveway.

"I don't get it," Peter said, leaning across the seat to speak through the open car door. "All this time we've thought he was hooked on fishing. Now we find out there was another attraction. But if she's moving away, why are you worried about the old man? She's driving right out of his life."

Henry looked toward a group of people who were gathered on the lawn close to the small yellow house, then looked back at his brother. "Because," he said, "G.H. doesn't want her traveling by herself. He's worried about her, and I'm afraid he'll go with her or do something equally crazy just to protect her. I suppose I'm humoring the old man *and* keeping his checkbook intact."

"Better you than me." Peter grinned. "Do you think this is the right house?"

Henry pulled a piece of paper out of his pocket. "Yup. This is it." He slammed the passenger door.

Peter rolled down the window and revved the car's engine. "Have a great trip," he called. "Don't forget to write."

Henry watched until the little red car disappeared around the corner, then tossed his jacket over his shoulder and picked up his bag and magazine with his good hand. A sandy-haired boy broke away from a group of children and ran over to him.

"Hi," he said panting. "Who are you?"

"Henry—Mr. Myles."

"Oh." The kid looked surprised. "I'd better go tell Mom you're here. We've been waitin'."

Mom? Henry's heart sank as he watched the boy run to the back of the house. G.H.'s blond "friend" couldn't be a mother, could she? Even G.H. couldn't expect Henry to travel across the country with a woman and a little boy. Henry realized the people on the lawn were regarding him with curiosity. Perspiration beaded on his forehead. He stood awkwardly in the driveway for a moment, then walked toward the crowd, thinking it was about time he met Jessica Whalen.

"HE'S HERE, MOM." Jeremy stood in the kitchen doorway and bounced on sneakered feet. His thick hair was stuck to his forehead and his cheeks were red from the sun. "You know, the guy who needs a ride?"

"Okay." His mother nodded, wiping her nose with a tissue. "Tell him I'll be right out." Jess sat on the kitchen floor with her back against the pine cabinets, a box of tissues beside her, while her best friend trimmed her bangs.

"Hold still. I'm almost done," Gayle said. "I wish you'd let me give you a perm last week when I wanted to."

The statement didn't require an answer. In her attempts to glamorize Jess's thick hair Gayle had been saying the same thing for two years. Jess tried not to sniff, although the sinus infection she was attempting to survive was in full bloom. "This is so pathetic."

Gayle scooted back and surveyed Jess's forehead. "You won't get an argument from me. I think you're crazy."

Jess stood up and turned on the kitchen faucet. She scooped water with her hands and splashed her face. "Oh, damn. There's nothing to dry with. I tossed the rest of the paper towels in the car."

"Here." Gayle handed her a wad of tissues. "Use these."

"Thanks." She quickly dried her face.

"It's not too late to change your mind, you know."

Jess tried to laugh, but the sound resembled a sob. She looked around the small kitchen. Empty except for a couple of plastic garbage bags, it looked abandoned and ugly. "No wonder I couldn't sell this place. Not much of a house, is it?"

Gayle shrugged. "I've seen worse."

"Not much of a life, either."

"Jess…" There was a sympathy in the word.

"It's true." She tossed the wet tissue into a trash bag. "All downhill since Tom died. Waitresses don't get rich."

"Neither do hairdressers, especially not in Idaho." She tucked her scissors into her purse. "But we don't all move to New England."

Jess sighed. How could she explain it to anyone, even her good friends? They thought she was in the middle of a nervous breakdown. All she really wanted to do was support her family. She cleared her throat and headed for the door. "It's for the best."

"Wait a minute." Gayle put her hand on Jess's shoulder and gave her a hug. Her voice was rough. "I'm rootin' for you, hon. I hope you get everything you want."

Jess felt her throat tighten, and fresh tears burned her eyes. "Thanks."

"But think about it, Jess." Gayle stepped back and stared hard into Jess's eyes. "Are you sure you want to travel with someone you don't even know? There's a strange person out there."

Jess tucked the tissue box under her arm. "Not so strange. He's the grandson of one of my customers. He needs a ride and I'll have someone who'll share the expenses. It should work out just fine. The only answers I got from the ad were a little weird."

"And this isn't?" Gayle stopped Jess at the door. "You don't even know the kid. You've only talked to him on the phone, right? How do you know what you're getting into?"

"I don't." She wiped her wet cheeks and laughed. "Actually, I've only talked to the old man's secretary. She had to leave a message at the café because I had the phone disconnected last week."

Gayle muttered a short oath. "You *have* lost your mind."

"No," she said. A deep shuddering breath helped her get her emotions under control. "C'mon, Gayle. I'm thirty-one years old. It's now or never." She gave her friend a wan smile. "Instead of being the oldest living waitress in north Idaho I'm going to be a rich and successful real estate agent, and I'm going to live by the ocean and eat lobster whenever I want to."

"You used to be so practical."

"I haven't changed." Jess wiped her nose. "C'mon, I've got to hit the road. If I don't get out of here soon I'll break down and cry for hours and never leave." She slipped her hand into the pocket of her baggy khaki shorts. "Here's a key to the house. Marty's daughter is going to come in and clean before the renters move in."

Gayle took the key and tossed it on the counter. "Okay. Anything else?"

Jess shook her head. "I hope not."

"Then this is it. You've probably had the car packed for days."

"Almost. I donated a lot of stuff to charity after the yard sale and put a few special things in Marty's garage. She'll mail them to us when we're settled somewhere. It just wasn't worth spending money renting a truck." Jess pushed the door open and went out into the afternoon sunshine.

Goodbye, house. Jess walked around the back of the house toward the driveway. She felt terrible. Her head ached and her eyes hurt in the bright sunlight. She didn't know how it was possible to have a nose that dripped twenty-four hours a day, but she had one. Her upper lip was raw from the constant use of tissues. Medication, aside from the antibiotic her doctor had prescribed, helped but made her sleepy and crabby, so she didn't take it. The last thing her kids needed was a cranky mother for three thousand miles. Or worse, a mom who fell asleep at the wheel.

Jess spotted the stranger right away. He stood near the back of the car, duffel bag in one hand, white sling cradling the other, a magazine rolled under his good arm. He was one of the best-looking men Jess had ever seen, and he looked as if he were getting ready to fly first-class instead of traveling several thousand miles in her old silver-blue Chevy.

"My goodness," said Gayle. "I assumed he was a college student."

"We assumed wrong," Jess said. She watched as he frowned and kicked one of the car's tires.

"He's handsome, but he looks a little…aggravated." Gayle grabbed Jess's elbow. "Are you sure you want to travel with him? I'll drive him back to Spokane or put him on a plane to Seattle. Just say the word and he's out of here."

Jess shook her head. A deal was a deal. She'd promised G.H. she'd help him. "Guess I'd better go introduce myself." Tears threatening once again, Jess firmly tucked the box of tissues under her arm and braced herself.

But there was suddenly no time to greet her passenger. Her friends surrounded her, taking turns saying goodbye with hugs, kisses and tears. Gayle's husband opened the car door for Jess, and she stood watching while the children climbed into the back seat of the crowded station wagon. Jess checked to make sure her tote bag and sunglasses were on the seat and looked across the roof of the car to G.H.'s grandson.

"Get in," she said, her voice cracking.

He didn't move. He stared at her and then toward the children inside the car. "Shouldn't we—"

"No," she said, a sob in her voice. "Just get in the damn car, *please*, before I change my mind."

His mouth formed a grim, angry line. He obviously didn't like being given orders, she noted. Tough. If she didn't get out of here she would break into a zillion pieces. She slid behind the wheel and hugged Gayle through the open window one last time. "I'll write, I promise."

"Take good care of yourself, Jess."

She started the car, put it in reverse, backed out of the driveway and quickly drove to the main road out of town. The only sounds were from the children sobbing in the back seat.

Sue wailed, "I want to go home, I want to go home!" and Jeremy sniffled softly and rhythmically near his mother's shoulder. Jess cried and drove east on Highway 200, fresh tears welling every time she thought of leaving her home and friends and setting off for the unknown. She forgot about the man beside her and concentrated on wiping her eyes in order to see the road.

"Any air-conditioning?" His voice rumbled when he spoke.

She shook her head, too choked up to speak, and drove past the eastern edge of Lake Pend Oreille and on through the sleepy town of Clark Fork.

"Excuse me," the man said. "Don't you think you ought to pull over?"

"Why?"

"Because you can't possibly see while you're crying."

"I'll be better in a minute." Jess hoped saying the words would make it true.

A long minute passed. "If you feel so badly, why are you leaving?" There was no patience or sympathy in his voice.

"Because," she began, but the tears overflowed once again. She waved one hand at him as if to say "forget it" and reached for another tissue.

But Henry wouldn't quit. "I don't relish being wrapped around a tree or splashed into the Clark Fork River because you can't keep your emotions under control."

Jess didn't think that deserved an answer. There was silence from the back seat. "Jeremy?" Jess asked, peering into the rearview mirror.

"Yeah?"

"Are you feeling better?"

"I'm just sad," he whispered.

"Me, too. What about Sue?"

"She's asleep."

"Good."

"And I'm hungry."

Jess nodded. "We'll stop in Thompson Falls and have lunch."

"My name is Henry Myles," Henry said loudly. "And I—"

"Look, Henry," Jess interrupted. "I'm not capable of carrying on a conversation right now, so I'm just going to keep crying until we get to the next town. We'll talk then, okay?" Out of the corner of her eye she saw him open up his magazine.

She drove toward Montana along the winding two-lane road that followed the path of the river that was always beside them. The waters of the Clark Fork tumbled toward Idaho, and Jess had the odd feeling that she was heading the wrong way, as if the river were right and she was traveling in the wrong direction. Going against the grain. She gripped the steering wheel with damp palms and leaned forward. The back of her cotton shirt was soaked with perspiration, and the air from the window gave little relief. A large wooden sign up ahead said Welcome to Montana. Jess's spirits lightened. She'd taken the first step and that had been the hardest.

Henry frowned at the sign. *Welcome to Hell might be more accurate,* he thought. Not that he had anything against Montana, but riding into it in a twenty-year-old heap with two crying children and a woman with severe emotional problems was not his idea of a perfect vacation. Henry was disgusted with himself. Damn G.H. anyway. Obviously the woman beside him was in no shape to make a trip across the United States. Every time she took her hand off the wheel to blow her nose he felt tense. He didn't know who she was or why she mattered to his grandfather, except that G.H. had always preferred his women young and blond. However this one wasn't as well endowed as G.H.'s women usually were. He glanced over at Jess again. She did have beautiful thighs, though, and her legs were smooth and tanned. Henry was a sucker for a great pair of legs.

She was ignoring him, and that was just fine with Henry. If they could ignore each other for the whole trip it might be bearable. The heat trapped in the car wasn't. Henry fumbled underneath the dashboard and found a vent. When he pulled it, warm air surrounded his feet. He settled back and flipped the pages of *Newsweek* to the economic forecast, his fingers sticking to the slick paper.

"Jer?"

"Yeah, Mom?"

"Is Harrigan out of the sun?"

"Who's Harrigan?" Henry asked, suspecting that, with his luck, there was an untrained puppy curled up in one of the cardboard boxes in the back of the car.

Jeremy shot an anxious look in Henry's direction and then answered his mother. "He's okay. I put his blanket over him."

"Who's Harrigan?" Henry repeated, staring at Jess's profile.

"The bird," she said.

"The bird." Henry supposed that was better than a puppy, but then envisioned green droppings on his shoulder. "I hope the bird is in a cage?"

Jess shot him an odd look. "Where else would he be? On the roof of the car?"

"There's no reason to be sarcastic."

"You're right." She sniffed. "I'm sorry. I'm having a hard day."

The understatement of the summer, Henry thought. He stared at Jess's red nose. A cute nose, if you liked Christmas carols. He wondered if an attempt to make pleasant conversation was in order. "Are you feeling better?"

"Yes." She smiled a little. "Thank you."

"Good. I was afraid you were so overcome with grief you'd plunge us headfirst into the river."

The smile faded. "Give me a break, Mr. Myles."

He was hopeless at pleasant conversation. "Oh, you heard my name? Good. Now that the polite introductions are over, could we discuss this trip?"

"There's no reason to be sarcastic, remember?" she shot back. "Besides, I have to concentrate. I hate driving."

"Then why aren't you flying to wherever it is you're going?"

"That's the problem," she said with a sigh. "I don't know where we're going. And I'll need a car when we get there."

Henry was silent. This woman was a complete flake. Not that he was any expert on women. Growing up without a mother or sisters had left him with little exposure to the intricate mental processes of the female mind. He envied Peter's ability to talk to anyone about any subject. Solitary Henry preferred to be alone. It was easier and less complicated. That is, until today, trapped in a station wagon with a woman, two sniffling kids and a bird.

Jess decided to pass the lumbering motor home she'd been following for miles and stepped on the gas pedal. When she had eased into the right lane again, she said, "What about you? Why aren't you flying to New York? Or taking the train?"

Good question. Henry knew he had to think fast. How could he say he was determined to protect his grandfather from any gold-digging plans she might have? "I'm afraid of flying."

"What about Amtrak?"

"Claustrophobia," he growled. "Can't breathe in trains."

"Oh. Well, I'm glad your grandfather could, uh, arrange a ride for you. It must be very hard not to be able to drive a car."

"It's hell." At least he could agree with her on something.

Jess drove in silence until they approached a small town, where she eased her foot off the gas pedal and looked around. "There," she said, pointing. "Mom's Cookin'. Doesn't that sound good?" She didn't wait for an answer, but swung the car into a shady parking space across the street from the restaurant.

Mom's Cold Beer would have sounded even better, Henry thought. It had to be more than 100 degrees outside. "Where are we?"

"Thompson Falls." She switched off the car engine and turned to look into the back seat. "Jer, wake up Sue, will you? And be gentle."

"Okay."

Sue sat up and blinked sleepily at Henry. She had the same streaky blonde hair as her mother and brother, the same brown eyes and pink skin.

"Twins?" Henry asked.

"No. They're a year apart, but everyone thinks they're twins." She grabbed a wad of tissues from the box on the seat of the car and shoved it into her canvas tote bag. "C'mon, people. This is lunch."

"Excuse me," Henry said. "But should we stop now? We've only been traveling for an hour and a half.

Opening the door and stepping out onto the pavement was her answer. "You're welcome to wait in the car."

That didn't bear thinking about. He opened the door with his good hand and stepped out awkwardly. Then Henry followed Jess as she held the children's hands and crossed the empty street toward Mom's. The interior of the restaurant was dark and cool. Jess looked around and then headed for an empty wooden booth. Henry hung back.

"Let's all sit together," Jess said. "There are some things we should discuss."

Henry reluctantly slid onto the bench alongside Jeremy and directly across from Jess. She stuck out her hand. "I'm Jessica Whalen. Call me Jess."

With his left hand, he took the warm fingers she offered and was surprised at the strength of the clasp. "Henry Myles."

An elderly waitress set menus and icy water glasses on the table. Jess picked up her glass and drained it immediately. "So you're G.H.'s grandson."

"Yes," Henry said, picking up his glass.

"He's a sweetheart. One of my favorite customers."

Henry choked on the water he was trying to swallow.

Jess leaned forward. "Are you okay?"

"Fine," he gasped.

Jess continued on. "Next to me is Susan. She's six. You've already met Jeremy. He's seven. Don't wiggle, Jer. You'll hit Henry's arm."

"Mr. Myles," Henry corrected.

Jess raised an eyebrow. "Well, if you want to be formal about it..."

Henry felt foolish. "It doesn't matter. Henry, then." He took a bottle of aspirin from his shirt pocket and popped open the top with his thumb.

"Is your arm hurting you?" For the first time she noticed his pallor.

"The damn thing won't quit aching." He swallowed a couple of aspirin and drank more water.

"How did you break it?"

"Sailing accident."

"Oh." Jess had no experience with boats and wasn't too crazy about the water at all. "That's too bad."

The waitress came over, her pencil ready. "You folks ready to order?"

"Hamburgers and fries for the children and me." She looked at Henry expectantly.

"Same here," he said.

The waitress collected the menus. "Anything to drink?"

"Water's fine," Jess answered. "A pitcher would be great." She didn't want to waste her money on soda pop when water was available. Susan tugged on her mother's arm. Jess bent down to listen and then said, "Excuse us."

In the rest room, Sue hurried to one of the stalls and Jess turned to the sink to splash water on her face. She tried not to look at herself in the mirror, and fortunately the glass was grimy enough to blur her reflection. The cold water made her eyes feel better. She wished she could lie down on a soft bed with cold washcloths on her face, but Missoula was only a few hours away. The motel would be air-conditioned, with an ice machine, and there would be clean cool sheets on the bed. Heaven couldn't get much better than that, she decided. For a second she thought of Henry and his aching arm. He was probably as anxious to get to Missoula as she was. She dried her face with a scratchy paper towel and glanced at the mirror. She looked worse than she'd imagined. Not that it mattered. She sure wasn't getting ready for the Mrs. America pageant.

When Jess and Sue returned to the booth, Jeremy was busy drawing designs on the paper napkin while Henry looked stiff and uncomfortable. Jess rummaged through her tote before sliding into the booth. "Here," she said, pushing a road atlas across the table. "I've outlined our route. Montana's right there on top."

Henry slowly reached for it and turned it around so he could see the highway highlighted in pink. "Is this the fastest way to New York?"

"I think so. That's where you're going isn't it?"

"I hope so." He watched her refill her glass. "And you're moving to New England?"

"Yep. To either Connecticut or Rhode Island. I'm not sure."

He decided not to make a comment about her lack of planning. It was none of his business if the woman didn't even know what state she was moving to. "I assume we'll be staying in Missoula tonight?"

She nodded. "I made reservations at a motel there."

"Good." He looked at his watch. "It's almost one-thirty, and Missoula's three hours away."

"Two-thirty. We lost an hour when we crossed the Montana border."

"Oh." He'd have to remember that. There was no way he could change the time on his watch with one hand.

"I guess your grandfather didn't tell you you'd be traveling with small children."

"That's correct." He slid the map back to Jess. "I assume they'll be quiet." Henry knew he sounded like a pompous ass, but he had no idea what to expect from little kids.

Jess looked irritated. "They're children. Well-behaved children who are very good travelers. Do you have a problem with that?"

The children looked at their mother and then stared at Henry. "We brought our Walkmans," Jeremy said, as if that solved Henry's problem.

He cleared his throat. "What about the financial arrangements?"

Jess brightened. He didn't look as if he was going to hitch a ride back to Idaho. "We'll each put fifty dollars in the envelope in the glove compartment for gas and oil. When that runs out we'll put in another fifty. That seems easiest."

He nodded. "All right."

"And we'll each take care of our own motel rooms and food. But I pick."

"Why?"

"I have a tight budget and the most people to feed, so I think that makes sense."

The waitress arrived with plates piled high with food and set them down on the table. "You folks must be travelin'."

Jess nodded and grabbed the road atlas off the table. "We sure are."

The woman peered at Jess's face. "Well, cheer up, honey. It can't be all bad." She plunked a plastic bottle of ketchup in the middle of the table. "At least you get to eat out."

"True." Jess chuckled. "Thanks."

"Sure, hon. You folks need anything else? No?" She tossed the check on the table. "Have a good trip."

Jess passed the ketchup to the kids and let them fix their hamburgers themselves. The burgers were large and juicy, the buns thick and dotted with sesame seeds. She wished she could smell the fries. She looked over at Henry. He was trying unsuccessfully to lift his hamburger. Not wanting him to think she was staring, she averted her eyes and focused on shaking some ketchup onto her plate. She could sense his frustration, though, and finally couldn't stand it any longer. "How about if I cut it in half for you?"

He frowned at her and wiped his hand on a napkin.

"Look," she ventured, "it might help."

"All right," he said, and almost smiled. "It's worth a try."

He pushed his plate over to her and Jess cut the hamburger in two. Then she pressed it down with the palm of her hand to flatten the bun. "There. Now you should be able to get a better grip on it." She pushed the plate back to him.

He eyed it suspiciously. "Thanks."

"You're welcome." Jess felt more cheerful as she picked up her hamburger and began to eat. The food was good, the water was cold, and although she and the kids looked puffy eyed, at least no one was crying.

From beneath lowered lashes she watched Henry grasp his hamburger. With swollen fingers he looked very uncomfortable. Since G.H. had called only three days ago to tell her he'd found a passenger she figured that Henry's accident must have been very recent. But Jess's reasons for not wanting to antagonize him weren't altogether humanitarian. She barely had enough money to make the trip by herself, and anything she could save would help at the other end. As it was, she was going to have to waitress while learning the ropes with a real estate company.

Jess ate her hamburger and dreamed of the future. Maybe she'd meet someone to share her life with. Someone who was fun, who could relax and laugh. Henry was a great-looking man—tall, dark and handsome—but the guy never smiled. At least he hadn't in the past hour. Moody Henry wasn't her type.

She wanted a man who would share the responsibilities of caring for her family, not that she'd ever admit it to anybody. Deep down she was tired of coping with everything by herself, from the blown circuit breaker to the weekly paycheck. She darted another look at the silent man across the table. Henry Myles was much too somber for love.

"Great fries, Mom. Better 'n Idaho," Jeremy said.

"Really?" She swallowed the last bite of her burger and then ate a french fry. "You're right."

"What's after Missoula?" Henry said.

Jess's mind went blank. "What?"

"Where will we stop the next day—Billings or Bozeman?"

"I guess that depends on how far we get."

"I don't have a lot of time." He frowned, his dark eyes serious. "This *will* be a quick trip, won't it?"

"As quick as it can be," she said through gritted teeth. Did he think she had the extra money to gallivant around the United States buying souvenirs?

"Good."

Jess looked down at her plate and attacked the rest of the french fries. *Don't antagonize him. Think of something pleasant. Stop feeling sorry for yourself.*

"Are you divorced?" Henry asked suddenly.

"Widow."

"I'm sorry."

"Me, too." Tom had been a loving husband who loved her with tenderness, if not wild passion. But she figured passion was overrated anyway.

"Any family?"

"Why the sudden interest, Mr. Myles?"

He flushed. "Just curious, I guess."

"My husband's mother lived in Sandpoint and died

shortly after Tom." Jess looked off into the distance. "I like to think of them together now, playing their favorite game of Scrabble. They would always try to cheat." Tears welled up in her eyes and she quickly wiped them away. "So now it's just the three of us."

"It's okay, Mom," Jeremy said. "You don't have to worry. We'll be real good in the car."

"I know that." She smiled at her children, noting that Sue had ketchup on her cheek. "You guys are great."

Sue shot a cautious glance at Henry before venturing to console her mother. "Cheer up, honey," she said, perfectly mimicking their waitress. "At least you get to eat out."

"She speaks!" Henry announced.

Jess laughed. "When she has something so say."

"Well," he said, wiping his hands with a napkin, "there's nothing wrong with that."

2

JESS WAS RELUCTANT to leave the cool interior of the restaurant; it felt like home. If it had been situated beside Lake Pend Oreille it would have been a sister to the café where she'd spent the past three years, pouring coffee and serving food to hungry tourists and fishermen. But it was time to move on.

After Jess and Henry examined the check and paid for lunch, they returned to the station wagon. Jess buckled her seat belt, wincing as the heat of the metal burned her fingers. "How's Harrigan, Jer?"

"Fine, Mom. He's in the shade."

She watched Henry turn toward the back of the car to get a glimpse of the bird. "A parakeet? You think that little bird's going to make it all the way to Connecticut?"

"Of course he is." She couldn't have left Harrigan behind in Idaho. His cheerful antics had buoyed her spirits when there hadn't been many reasons to laugh.

"He'll never make it."

"Mom?" Jeremy hung over the front seat while Jess started the car. "Is that true?"

Jess glared at Henry. "Mr. Myles, are you some sort of bird expert?"

"Do you mean an ornithologist?"

"Whatever."

"Well, no."

She turned to her son. "There's your answer, Jer. Mr.

Myles doesn't understand what a good friend Harrigan is to us."

"All I said—" Henry began.

"Forget it," she said, putting the car into reverse. "Next stop is the jail."

"What jail?" Henry said.

"You'll see when we get there."

Thirty minutes later Jess drove into Plains, a small railroad town. She swung the car north onto a narrow side street and searched for a building she was certain would impress the children. Her other companion could stay in the car if he wanted to.

"There it is," she said, pointing.

"There what is?" All he saw was a very old, very small building. Stone, with small barred windows, it sat on a dusty square of grass.

"Wow!" the kids said in unison.

"Pretty neat, huh?" Jess opened the car door. "Come on. We'll take a couple of pictures so you can show all your new friends."

"What new friends?" Susan asked.

"All the ones you're going to make in our new home."

"Oh." But the child didn't seem convinced. Her eyes filled with tears. "I just want Amy."

Jess hugged her. "Come on. We'll get some cold drinks, too."

Henry approved. The heat was still heavy, the sun burning relentlessly in the clear Montana sky. Cold drinks—and plenty of them—sounded like just what he needed. He eyed the building and unzipped his duffel bag to grab his camera. He might as well get a picture of the jail. Who knew when he'd ever see something like this again?

Jess posed the kids by the building and aimed her small plastic camera as if she were photographing a cover for *People* magazine. Henry frowned with impatience, then waited until the kids had raced around the back of the building; he wanted an unobstructed picture of the jail.

Handling the camera with his left hand was harder than he'd thought it would be. It took several tries before he was able to focus. Luckily his hands were big enough to hold the camera steady while he pushed the shutter release. He would tell G.H. that this was a place where dirty old men were sent after getting involved with pretty young blondes.

Henry watched Jess walk toward the back of the building to call the kids. She had great legs. Even though her skin was creased by the vinyl seat of the car, the shape was there. And her cute bottom in those baggy shorts was only hinted at, but he was willing to bet it matched the rest of her. Guess he couldn't blame G.H. too much, but the man should have had better sense than to let himself be bamboozled by a sweet-talking lady who probably put on a helpless act every time old men came near.

Henry got back in the car, which was like an oven. He looked over the back seat to see the green-and-yellow parakeet sitting serenely on his perch. The bird looked up at Henry. "Eep."

"Better enjoy your last remaining days, bird," Henry muttered.

Jess and the kids came back to the car.

"That was neat, Mom."

"Yeah," Sue agreed.

"Well, we needed a break." Jess smiled at Henry as if he agreed with her, then turned away when he said nothing.

They drove out of town and found a gas station combined with a convenience store. "What does everyone want to drink?" Jess asked.

"Root beer," said Jer.

"Me, too," Sue said.

"Henry?"

Henry would have liked to put his broken arm on top of a pan of ice and lie naked in an air-conditioned motel room. "Cola. Large." He reached for his pants pocket.

"Forget it," she said. "I'll treat."

"No." He pulled out a fat black wallet and opened it on his thigh. He handed a five-dollar bill to Jess. "Get me two, please."

He'd said please. Jess thought that deserved trumpets. "Okay," she agreed, taking the bill. "Anybody have to go to the bathroom?"

The kids tumbled out of the car. "Can we buy a postcard for our scrapbooks?"

"Sure." Jess was glad the children weren't crying anymore. The trip was supposed to be fun, an adventure, not a funeral procession. Once more, heavy sadness at the thought of leaving her home and friends enveloped her, but she swallowed the lump in her throat and blinked back tears. Strong. She had to be strong.

She bought the drinks, making two trips and delivering Henry's colas first. He didn't seem to want to go to the bathroom.

"Well, on to Paradise," Jess said, getting back behind the wheel of the car.

Henry shot her a wry look. "Aren't you being overly optimistic?"

She grinned. "Paradise, Montana, Mr. Myles. It's a town just a few miles from here." He didn't answer and Jess had the satisfaction of getting in the last word.

They stopped two more times for something cold to drink, and Jess began to think she was crazy for traveling during the hottest part of the day. She resolved to buy a cooler in Missoula and continued to negotiate the twisting two-lane road, thankful for the giant fir trees that appeared at intervals to shadow the sun. At this point she was grateful for the smallest kindness. Even from trees.

In a sleepy little town called Alberton, whose sign claimed the world's largest used bookstore, the four travelers sat in a dark saloon and drank soda. The two other customers didn't seem to mind that the kids were there; it was probably only a saloon at night, Jess reasoned. Besides, it seemed to be the only place in town to get a drink of any kind, except for the vending machine on the side of the wooden gas station.

Jess was reluctant to get back into the car. "Let's go into the world's largest bookstore."

"Why?" Henry sat on a padded red chair and leaned on the dingy Formica table. He was contemplating ordering a cold draft beer in a frosty mug. He looked past Jess's shoulder to the sign that advertised draft beer—a dusty neon waterfall foaming past a watching moose.

"*Used* bookstore," Sue said.

Jess shrugged. "Books are books."

"That's a profound thought," Henry muttered.

"Thank you." She stood and threw three dollars onto the table. "Tell you what. I'm going to walk down the street and look at the bookstore. I don't even know if it's open. Anyone who wants to come can. Otherwise stay here for another fifteen minutes or wait in the car with Harrigan." She'd parked in the shade of a tree, and the windows were cracked open enough to let air in.

No one moved.

"We'll stay here with him," Jeremy said, pointing to Henry.

Sue nodded. "Yeah."

Henry didn't looked too pleased and neither was Jess. She hesitated. What if the man was a child molester? From what she'd heard on television lately, not all molesters wore raincoats and had three-day-old beards. Some were pillars of their communities. It was impossible to tell.

Henry gave her an odd look. "They'll be fine."

"Well..." The man was G.H.'s grandson, after all. Surely G.H. wouldn't ask her to travel with a pervert. She really didn't want to look at books—used or otherwise—now, but Henry glared at her as if he knew what she was thinking and would like to strangle her for it. "I won't be long, maybe five minutes."

"Fine."

She pulled two more one-dollar bills from her wallet and gave them to the kids. "Buy yourselves another drink."

She left the saloon, turned right along the broken sidewalk and felt like the worst mother in the world. But at least she had the car keys. He couldn't steal her car and her kids and abandon her in Alberton, Montana. Besides, he wouldn't want to steal her kids, of that she was certain. He didn't appear to be the parental type. He probably dated tall, elegant women who knew how to sail those skinny sleek boats. She pictured Henry with the type of woman who could pose for one of those "Office to Evening Wear" articles, someone who could whip off pieces of a business suit and become a glamorous woman on the prowl...all in ten minutes in the corporate ladies' room.

Lord, it was hot. Just walking a block made her feel as if she needed a shower. Even the wind was hot, and it blew dust around her, but, she thought, a breeze was a breeze. She pushed open the door of the bookstore, a converted house, which seemed to be empty. No one appeared as the bell tinkled on the door closing behind Jess. From floor to ceiling were shelves of books, with barely enough aisle space between them for a thin person to pass through. Cardboard labels were thumb-tacked to the walls.

It was heaven for a bookworm like Jess. She felt her worries ease for a moment as she reveled in the sight of all the books. She savored the quiet. She took a deep breath and enjoyed the first free minute she'd had in a very long time.

She roamed through the aisles of the store, enjoying the sight of all those books crammed together. She took one off the shelf and flipped to the inside cover. The penciled price was a fair one, definitely a discount over the usual hardcover cost. It was soothing, she thought, to be in the midst of all these books. There had been little time for reading in the past years, although when the children were little and Tom was alive, she would spend many hours curled up near the wood stove in the living room, reading mysteries and romances and popular fiction until early in the morning.

How would her life change now? For the better, she hoped fervently.

The dust made her sneeze and she reached in her pocket for a tissue to blow her nose. Things were changing. They were changing because she'd made them change. Better or worse.

"May I help you?" An elderly woman stood at the foot of the A–C aisle.

"Oh, I'm just looking," Jess said, an apology in her voice.

"Good. That's what everyone does. It's what we're here for. If you find something you want just bring it to the desk. The paperbacks are downstairs. And if there's anything special you're looking for, we can call our main store in Pennsylvania."

"Thank you." Jess roamed through the stacks and then followed red arrows on the walls to the basement stairs. She knew she should take only a few minutes more, but it was tempting to look at the paperbacks. Maybe she'd find something she could read at night in the motels. She had to laugh at herself. She'd be driving hundreds of miles every day with two kids and an obnoxious injured passenger and she thought she'd have energy leftover to read at night? Who did she think she was kidding?

She went downstairs anyway and discovered two early Larry McMurtry paperbacks. She took them upstairs to the woman behind the desk. "How much?"

"Two dollars," she said. "And please take our card, in case you ever need a book searched for. We do that, too."

"Thanks, but I'm moving east. I don't think I'll be this way for a long time." The words sounded funny, as if they were being spoken by someone else. She rummaged through her bag for the money.

"Oh? Where are you from?"

"Idaho," she said. Then realizing how broad a statement that was, added, "Near Sandpoint. On Lake Pend Oreille."

The woman nodded. "I've heard of it. Do you need a bag?"

Jess shook her head and tucked the books into her tote.

"Well, have a nice trip."

"Thanks." Jess turned and walked to the door, anxious to get on her way. Missoula couldn't be too much farther now. She walked along the broken sidewalk to the saloon and went inside. Henry sat in the same place—alone.

Her heart skipped a beat. "Where are the kids?"

"In the bathroom. For the fifth time." He didn't look perturbed about it. "Are we ready to go?"

She hesitated, then sat down. "As soon as they come back."

"Good." He pulled some bills from his wallet and placed them on the table.

Jess saw him wince. "How's your arm?"

"Not so good." He studied her as she watched the back of the saloon. She had beautiful hair, the thick kind a man liked to lift from a woman's shoulders before he kissed her nape. "You have dirt on your face," he snapped.

Jess turned back to him, surprised. "Oh?" Her voice was mild. She took a napkin from the table. "Where?"

"Your right cheek."

Jess rubbed her face. "Guess the books were dustier than I knew. Better?"

He nodded. It was too bad about her looks. He wished she'd put her sunglasses back on. "How was the world's largest bookstore?"

"I bought a couple of paperbacks." Jess saw the kids coming and stood up. "Air-conditioning, here we come."

JESS UNLOCKED the door of number 31 and pushed it open to reveal a blue room with two queen-size beds and a typical assortment of motel furniture. The air was stale, but cool. It was heaven, Jess decided. Well, maybe not heaven, because the air conditioner needed to be cranked up, but close enough—there wasn't a steering wheel in sight. Her eyes hurt and her eyelids drooped, but she couldn't collapse yet. Sue was busy opening every dresser drawer while Jeremy stood at the window and looked outside toward the pool.

"Can we go swimming now?" he asked.

"In a few minutes," Jess told him. "After we finish unloading the car." She set the bird cage on top of the dresser, making sure it wasn't in a draft. Harrigan peered at her and squawked. "Hello, baby," Jess crooned, hoping the bird would return the greeting.

He squawked again.

"Hello, baby," she repeated. One of these days Harrigan would have to speak. Jess waited, but he lifted his wings and remained silent.

"C'mon, Mom. Let's go." Jeremy urged. "That pool looks so neat."

The three of them made one more trip down the outside cement stairs to the parking area and took food and luggage from the station wagon. The parking lot was U-shaped, surrounding the fence-enclosed pool on three sides. Behind the wire, several people splashed in the water.

"I can't wait," Jeremy moaned. "I'm so hot."

"I know." Jess sniffed. Out of breath and more than a little dizzy, she headed toward the stairs. "C'mon, kids. Just one more time."

They trudged back to their room.

"Where's Henry?" Sue asked.

"He went to his room, I guess," Jess replied. He had registered after her and hadn't bothered to tell her what room he was in. She guessed he didn't think it important to be able to get in touch. She hid her irritation from the children and unlocked the door. "He looked tired."

"Yeah," her daughter said. "Maybe that's why he didn't smile."

"His arm hurts," Jeremy said.

Sue frowned. "All *day*?"

"You'd be screamin' your head off if *you* had a broken arm," Jeremy said.

"I'm going to scream my head off if you two don't get into this room," Jess told them. "You're letting the hot air in."

Sue obeyed her mother, but kept talking. "I think Henry's a grump."

"I don't think he's too crazy about us, either," Jess

said. "So don't worry about it, okay?" Jess could hardly breathe as she took another antibiotic capsule. She longed to lie down on the inviting expanse of blue bedspread, but it took the children only a few minutes to change into their bathing suits.

Jeremy ran to the door. "C'mon, Mom."

"Okay," Jess said, sighing. "Let me find my suit."

Sue fished a bathing suit out of Jess's tote bag and dangled it in front of her mother. Jess stood and took it into the bathroom to change. She didn't know why she was putting on her suit—it had something to do with being a mother and being ready to dive in to save her kids from drowning. Unless there was an emergency, she certainly didn't plan to swim.

"Take towels," Jess told the kids. She grabbed the room key and her purse, then followed the children outside. Around the corner, at the bottom of the stairway, she paused at the soda machine to buy a cold can of diet cola. She held it against her forehead, hoping the cold would numb her aching temples, then took Sue's hand and crossed the parking lot. There was another young family at the pool, with a toddler supported by a life jacket. He paddled happily around his parents.

"Can we go in now?" Sue asked.

Jess nodded. "Be careful not to splash the little guy over there." She spread a towel on a heavy metal lounger, kicked off her sandals and sat down. "Don't go over your head," she added. "I'll probably get pneumonia if I have to rescue you."

"We won't!" Jeremy agreed. They both wore silly grins as they slid off the edge of the pool into the water.

Jess opened the can of soda and took a long swallow. She knew the children were good swimmers; they'd been taking lessons since they were old enough to walk. She fished her sunglasses out of her bag and lay back on the lounger. The afternoon was still hot, but the heat was tempered by the smell of chlorine and the occasional spray of pool water.

Jess looked at her watch. Six. The kids could swim for an hour, she could order pizza delivered to the room, and they'd all be asleep by nine. And if this heat wave continued, it would be wise to be on the road early in the morning. Around five would be good. Jess liked that time for traveling anyway. Cool, dark and private—it was the best time to be on the road. Then there was the added benefit of watching the sun come up. Hot coffee from a truck stop, maybe some doughnuts to nibble on…

HENRY OPENED THE GATE to the pool area and shut it carefully behind him. The metal was hot to his fingers, but he didn't react. He'd taken a couple of pain pills when he reached his room and was starting to numb up now. A familiar voice yelled at Sue to get out of the way, and Henry's attention was drawn to the children in the water. He paused. He should have known they'd be there at the pool.

And there in the corner was Jess Whalen. She was stretched out on a lounge chair, her body relaxed and still. He couldn't tell for sure, because she wore sunglasses, but he guessed she was sound asleep. He wouldn't have minded a nap himself, but the pool had been irresistible. He wanted to sit on the edge and cool off his feet at least.

He looked back at Jess. She was a tempting sight, but he didn't want to ogle like some kind of pervert. Although any man in his right mind would have taken a second look at the shapely woman in a black one-piece suit, lying so provocatively in her chair. Her blond hair lay soft against her shoulders, and the sunglasses gave her a mysterious air. Her nose didn't look red from where he stood. Henry decided she looked better with her clothes off and at a distance. *Stay away,* he told himself. This woman made tough old men drool on their sweater vests.

He was determined not to drool on any clothing whatsoever. Jess Whalen was dangerous, off-limits and definitely not the most attractive woman he'd ever met in his life. Add to that two children and the general zaniness of this trip, and he should have been walking backward.

He stepped closer. Jeremy waved to him and Henry waved back. Perspiration beaded his chest, and he looked longingly at the sparkling water. He moved to the edge of the pool and carefully eased himself down onto the concrete. After he slid his feet into the water Henry knew he'd made the right decision in coming to the pool. Even the hot sun that pounded on his head didn't faze him, the combination of pain pills and cool water was such a soothing one.

He looked back over to Jess and wondered what she would do if these rambunctious kids of hers started to drown. Did she have a built-in safety mechanism that would wake her up? He hoped so. As a lifeguard, he wasn't worth much. He supposed he could supply mouth-to-mouth resuscitation if someone could get the victim on land.

Henry sighed as he watched Jeremy swim over to him.

"Hi," the child said.

"Hello."

"How's your arm now?"

"Better."

The boy gripped the edge of the pool and looked content to hang there beside Henry. "We're getting pizza for dinner. We're gonna order in to our room and watch cable."

"Good."

"You want some?"

"No, thanks." Henry had no desire to be crammed into an ugly motel room with his traveling companions and eat pizza that probably tasted not much better than its box. But he appreciated the invitation.

"Why not? Do you hate pizza or something?"

"Everyone likes pizza. I'm just not very hungry."

"Oh." Jeremy squinted up at the man as if he couldn't believe that anyone was ever not hungry. "How'd you hurt your arm?"

"I had an accident on my sailboat."

The child's eyes widened. "Wow! You have your own boat?"

Henry nodded. A lot of good it did him to have a boat this summer.

Sue paddled over and pulled herself out of the water to sit beside Henry. She eyed his cast and moved away several inches.

"Hurts, huh?" she said.

He nodded, then looked over at Jess. "Your mother's tired."

"She's not really asleep," Jeremy said, pulling himself onto the ledge to sit on Henry's other side. "She's just resting."

"Oh." Henry doubted that was true, even though the parking area was noisy as cars backed in and out, and a young couple was having a hell of a time trying to talk their screaming little kid into getting out of the pool. The kid's life jacket kept him bobbing on the water as he screamed, and Henry wished briefly that he would get a mouthful of water and be quiet for a moment or two. Henry, Jeremy and Sue watched as the father tried to cajole the child out of the water. His patience finally used up, the young man grabbed the child's life jacket and lifted him out of the pool to his mother. As they headed toward the gate, the father turned to Henry and smiled.

"Terrible twos!" he said. "It'll be nice when he's the age of your kids."

Henry nodded, too surprised to reply. He certainly was not going to explain to a total stranger that these two towheaded people did not belong to him. There was certainly no family resemblance.

"He thinks you're our dad," Jeremy said.

"Guess so," Henry replied.

Sue giggled and hopped back into the water.

"You're just gonna let him think that?" the boy persisted.

"C'mon, Jer, let's swim some more," his sister urged.

Jeremy ignored her and kept looking up at Henry. Henry was becoming decidedly uncomfortable. "What difference does it make?"

"I dunno." The child's voice was thoughtful. "It just does."

"It does?" Henry stalled. Why was he having this conversation? He squinted and looked over to Jess. She hadn't moved, still stretched out in dreamland while he was stuck answering questions about fatherhood. "I'm sorry."

Jeremy shrugged and looked away. He bit his lower lip.

"Come *on*, Jer!" Sue called, paddling to the other side of the pool. "We can race."

He hesitated, then hopped off the edge with a splash.

Henry moved his feet in the water. He had never been mistaken for a father before. He'd never spent much time around kids, either. Even his younger brother couldn't qualify, as Henry had been sent to private schools shortly after Peter's birth and the death of his mother.

School was a good place to be, and Henry had loved it. The house in Seattle had been dark and silent, filled with men and boys who didn't quite know what to do with themselves in their free time. It was better to be away from the house, where there was light and fun and other boys to play with.

Even now, although his lakefront town house was light and airy, with tall windows and white walls, the freedom and peace of being on the open water was his salvation after the long hours he spent at the office. And the women he chose to spend time with did not have red noses, blond children or old cars. They were not waitresses. They did not date his grandfather. They knew where they were going when they got behind the wheel of a car, or at least they looked as if they did.

And they were scary: determined, sure of themselves, totally confident and strong. Which was why it was easier to be out on the water by himself.

He wondered if he'd always be by himself. He looked over to Jess, who moved those beautiful legs, stretching out on the chaise in a slightly different position. Longing swept over him, and he didn't like himself for it. But he couldn't help it, he decided. He was only human. He was only a man sitting innocently on the edge of a pool watching a beautiful woman sleep. There were worse things to do on a hot day.

JESS SHIFTED POSITIONS. Her throat was dry, and she had a strong feeling that someone was staring at her. She sat up and opened her eyes, thankful for the sunglasses that helped hide her embarrassment. The kids were busy swimming, splashing happily in the water; it looked wonderful. If she wouldn't be risking pneumonia she'd have been in there with them. She reached for a tissue, wiped her nose, then took a drink. The soda wasn't very cold, but still soothed her throat.

Henry was sitting on the edge of the pool—there was no mistaking the dark hair and the white sling. He was more deeply tanned than she'd thought he would be, but then again he'd said something about a sailboat. Had he been the one staring at her? She had the uncomfortable feeling that he had, and that he hadn't been thinking anything kind.

Henry harbored some sort of animosity toward her, though she couldn't imagine why. He should have been happy to have a ride. Maybe he didn't like her kids. Or her car. With a wry smile she realized that the list was too long to mention after all.

He was definitely looking at her now, probably wondering why she was staring at him. She waved, as if they were good ol' buddies, sitting at the pool together.

She watched as he eased himself off the cement and walked over to her. Suddenly she felt uncomfortable being in her bathing suit; the daring cut of the legs had almost stopped her from buying it. But she relaxed when she saw Henry's face. Her thighs would certainly not be keeping him awake at night. He looked preoccupied, very serious, and his gaze never wavered from her face.

"What's the schedule for tomorrow?"

He had a nice body, strong legs and at least one surprisingly well-muscled arm. Lots of dark hair matted his chest, although his sling covered part of it. She cleared her throat and tried to look official. "I thought we'd get an early start."

"How early?"

"Five o'clock." She would have her Montana sunrise to look forward to. "I like to travel early in the morning."

He looked surprised. One dark eyebrow rose. "Sounds good to me."

"Great. I'll knock on your door when we're packing the car."

"Fine."

"What room?"

"Nineteen." He frowned. "But I'll be ready."

"Okay." She swung her legs over the edge of the lounger. "What a hot day. Too bad you can't swim."

He shrugged. "I guess I'd better get used to it. It'll be six weeks before this cast comes off." He stepped back so she could stand up.

"Do you have a doctor in New York?" she asked as she waved to the children to come out of the water.

"New York?" Henry had trouble keeping his gaze away from Jess's body. "Oh, sure. I'll find somebody. See you in the morning." He backed up a few more feet, then abruptly turned and headed toward the gate. New York seemed awfully faraway.

"PEPPERONI," Jess said into the telephone. "Thick crust." After giving the motel room number, she hung up the phone and turned to the kids.

"Jeremy asked Henry if he wanted pizza," Sue announced.

"What?" Jess sat in her underwear and T-shirt, ready for eating pizza in bed.

"He said no."

Jess relaxed. She wasn't up to entertaining, and she didn't want to change. She was still groggy from her nap by the pool, but dozing in the sun had been soothing. And knowing there was nothing left to do was wonderful. She wanted to savor the idea that there was nothing more to sell or pack, no one to say goodbye to, nothing to arrange or wash.... All she had to do was climb into the car each day and hit the road. "When did you talk to Henry?"

"At the pool, remember?"

"Oh."

"Yeah," Jeremy said, switching the channels on the television for the hundredth time. "He couldn't swim."

"No, I suppose not." She picked up one of her new books. *Moving On* was the title. Appropriate. She hoped it wouldn't get romantic.

3

JESS SURVEYED the motel room one last time before closing the door. Satisfied nothing had been left behind, she stepped onto the balcony and shut the door behind her. She took a deep breath of the cool morning air, glad she'd worn a sweatshirt and jeans.

"All set?" rumbled a voice behind her.

Jess jumped and looked up to see Henry standing near her, his bag in his hand. She had knocked on his door ten minutes ago, but hadn't waited for an answer.

"I was on my way to find you," he said, his voice low, "when I saw you coming out of the room. I stopped at the car first. The kids looked like they were going back to sleep."

Jess smiled. Maybe Henry would be easier to get along with today. "They were pretty tired this morning."

They walked down the stairs together and across the silent parking area to the car. The children were sleeping soundly in the back, where Jess had folded down the seat and spread sleeping bags to make a comfortable bed. She opened the door slowly, hoping the noise wouldn't disturb them. Henry imitated her quiet movements as he joined her in the front seat. A distracting sensation of intimacy filled the dark car, and Jess began to feel self-conscious.

"Do you drink coffee?" she whispered.

"Yes."

"I have a thermos under the seat. We'll stop and fill

it at one of the truck stops before we get on the interstate."

"You'll need gas."

"I know." Jess hid a yawn behind her hand, then pulled the keys from her jeans pocket. She switched on the ignition, but nothing happened. Disbelieving, she tried again. The engine ground uselessly, then made a dreadful slamming sound. Jess's stomach tightened. She didn't want to look at Henry, but could feel his gaze on her. She leaned back against the seat and waited.

He cleared his throat. "Great day for traveling."

Jess nodded, and reached forward to try the key again. This time the noise was worse. "I don't think we're going anywhere right away." She glanced toward Henry. Even in the darkness she could tell he looked disgusted. "Do you know anything about cars?"

He shook his head. "A few basics. Pull the hood latch and I'll do my best."

Moments later they stood in front of the car looking down at the black hole that held the engine.

"Do you have a flashlight?" His tone clearly stated he didn't imagine she would.

"Sure," she said, and went back to the car and pulled it from under the seat. It was long and silver, a gift from her worried friends. "There." She switched on the light to bathe the engine in a bright glow. "See anything?"

"This is ridiculous," he muttered. He wiggled a few connections. "Nothing's loose, anyway."

"That's good?"

"That's as good as it gets." He backed away. "I've surpassed my knowledge now."

"I thought guys took shop in high school."

"Where have you been? Girls do, too."

"Oh."

"We could clean off the spark plugs, but they look okay."

"I had the car checked before I left, just so something like this wouldn't happen."

The look he shot at her was not nice. "Stand back," he said, and slammed the hood shut with one strong hand. "You'll have to call a mechanic."

"It's Sunday."

"It's broken," he countered.

"I realize that." Was he acting deliberately nasty? After all, Henry was free to hop on a bus or a train—despite his dislike of those things—and head for New York. Unlike her. She could be stuck in Missoula for the rest of her life, trying to make enough money waiting tables to save up for another car. Jess decided that Henry Myles didn't have a handle on the real world. "What do you do?"

"What?"

"For a job. What do you do?"

Henry hesitated. This wasn't good. He didn't want her to know he was wealthy in his own right, although she probably assumed that already, because he was related to G.H. But he didn't want to encourage the fortune hunter in her. He had enough trouble in this car already. "I'm…between jobs right now."

"Oh." Jess decided to let it drop. He was obviously embarrassed, the poor guy. No wonder he was crabby. He was injured and out of work. She attempted to sound cheerful. "No wonder you get to sail so much."

He glared at her. "I'm not exactly a bum."

"Is that why you're going to New York? For a job?"

"I really don't want to discuss this. Right now talking about New York is a moot point, if you get my drift. We need to call a gas station." The neon lights of the motel's restaurant flickered on. "And have breakfast. Coffee to start with."

"I'd rather not wake up the kids right now."

"Good. We can go over to the restaurant, have some coffee, make phone calls." He wanted to take her elbow and steer her toward the restaurant, but settled for standing beside her.

"But the kids—"

"Are asleep. We'll sit by the window and if one of their heads pops up you can run over and tell them what's going on."

He sounded reasonable and his plan made sense, but Jess hesitated. She didn't want to sit in the restaurant with him, and she didn't want him involved with the fixing of her car. It was embarrassing to be stuck like this. And she wasn't sure she liked being bossed around. On the other hand, maybe Henry was only trying to be nice.

"Besides," he added, "the sooner we get this old crate fixed, the sooner this entire trip will be over."

So much for being nice, Jess thought. At least there could be no doubt where his feelings on the subject lay. Jess returned the flashlight to its place under the seat, peeked one more time at the children and locked the car doors before following Henry across the parking lot. They were the first customers in the restaurant, and Jess followed Henry to a booth by the window that faced the parking lot. A nearby streetlight cast a glow that clearly outlined the car. Jess sighed.

"All set?" Henry asked. He'd never dated a mother before. They seemed to worry a lot, especially about their children. However, this one didn't seem concerned that she had no makeup on, or that her hair hung straight. Although, he decided, she didn't look too bad. Her nose wasn't as red today.

"Yes, this is fine."

Henry smelled fresh coffee. He planned to drink at least a gallon of the stuff to counteract the side effects of the pain pills he'd taken last night.

The waitress came over with two cups and a plastic pot. "Coffee?"

Jess and Henry nodded, and the waitress put two menus on the table, poured the coffee and walked away. Henry studied the menu briefly, thinking that this was a hell of a lot better than balancing take-out coffee on the front seat of the car.

"Well, now what?" he said.

"I'll call a mechanic as soon as it's light." Jess took a swallow of coffee. Wonderful. She might just live. "With luck, someone will be able to look at the car this morning. It's tourist season. We can't be the only people in Missoula who've ever had car trouble on a Sunday."

"I'll get the keys to the rooms back from the guy at the desk," Henry offered.

The waitress returned. "Ready to order?"

Jess listened as Henry ordered an enormous amount of food.

"Ma'am?"

"Just an English muffin, please."

"That's it?" Henry frowned.

"I'm not very hungry this early in the morning," Jess said, dismissing the subject. "How's your arm today?"

"Better, I guess. I slept pretty well last night." He paused. "How's your nose?"

"Okay. A few more days of antibiotics and I should be as good as new." She looked out the window toward the car. The children hadn't popped up yet. They'd be surprised when they awoke and discovered they weren't even out of the parking lot.

Henry began to have more second thoughts about this trip. Sitting in a restaurant before sunrise with a strange woman was not exactly his idea of a good time. He tried to picture Jess on his sailboat. She seemed strong and capable enough to go sailing; she would probably pull her own weight, cook breakfast, and sun those gorgeous legs of hers on the deck. She sneezed and the vision dissolved. He had no reason—except protecting old G.H.'s checkbook—to be in this orange booth about to have breakfast with his grandfather's latest sweetie.

Jess considered her budget while she drank her coffee. The problem of what could be wrong with the car and how much it would cost to fix was a definite worry right now. No wonder the only food she could contemplate choking down was a muffin. The nerves in her stomach began to dance. Henry, though, looked content to anticipate his big breakfast. That annoyed her. "How do you usually travel," she asked, "if you hate to fly and you don't take the train? Do you always drive?"

"Always," Henry lied. He almost felt sorry for her.

Jess didn't know what to say to that. It sounded a little strange, but she supposed there were stranger things a person could be afraid of. She herself didn't like heights very much and wasn't too thrilled about cities—they made her feel claustrophobic. Henry had said trains made him feel that way. But if they'd been taking the train they'd be heading east by now and wouldn't have had to worry about finding a mechanic on a dark Sunday morning.

The waitress came to the table with the breakfast.

"Do you have a phone book I could borrow?" Jess asked.

"There's one underneath the telephone booth outside, but there's probably a chain on it."

Henry flashed the woman a charming smile. "If you

could do us a favor by finding the yellow pages somewhere, I'd be very grateful."

The waitress softened. "I could bring you one from the back, if you'll promise you won't walk off with it."

"That would be perfect," Henry said. "We've had car trouble and need to find a mechanic."

"Right-o," she said. "Here's jelly for the muffin."

"*We've* had car trouble?" Jess watched Henry arrange a plate of bacon and eggs, a side order of hash browns and glasses of orange juice and milk.

"I'm in the car, too. And I'm paying my way, if you'll remember."

The waitress returned with fresh coffee, a thick yellow book and a smile for Henry.

"Thanks," Jess said. She pushed her muffin aside and opened the book to search for a garage. "Automobile repairing," she muttered. "Good, there are a lot of ads."

"Any that mention twenty-four-hour service?"

She studied the pages. "Two."

"Good," he said, forking a piece of egg. "Try them first."

I knew that, Jess wanted to say, but she decided it wouldn't be wise to antagonize him before sunrise. She continued to study the ads, looking for one that would accept her brand-new credit card. She didn't like the damn thing, but it was to be used in an emergency. Her stomach tightened. This felt like an emergency. "Ray's Dependable Service Station," she read. "Seven-day, twenty-four-hour automotive repair, all major credit cards."

Henry managed to divert his attention from his breakfast long enough to nod. "Sounds like a good one to call."

"Dependable's a nice word." Jess sighed and drank her coffee.

Later, after she went outside to make the call and check on the sleeping children, she returned the phone book to the waitress and joined Henry in the booth. The dishes had been cleared from the tabletop, and Henry looked content to drink coffee and read the Sunday morning paper spread all over the table. He looked up from the business section. "What did Ray say?"

"I talked to someone at the gas station. Ray's off for the weekend, playing golf, but his cousin Eddie, the mechanic, will be here at eleven, after church."

"Eleven?" He put the paper down. "That's more than five hours from now." His eyes darkened to a deep shade of green.

Jess hadn't noticed the intriguing color of his eyes before. She'd been too busy trying to avoid looking at him, she supposed, because every time she did he was frowning at her.

She shrugged. "Short of kidnapping Eddie before he goes to church, I don't see what else we can do." She dug three dollars from her wallet. "Here's my share of the breakfast. I'm going to get the key and take the kids back to the room."

"Fine. Let me know when the car's fixed and you're ready to leave." He picked up the folded section of newspaper and continued to read.

So much for strong male support. Jess almost laughed. She didn't need him anyway. Aside from lifting the hood of the car, Henry hadn't been much help. He was making it clear that he was just a passenger, not to be involved in the day-to-day problems of driving from one point to another. He didn't even notice when she snitched the comics off the table.

Jess stepped outside and looked past the parking lot to the distant hills. The eastern sky grew lighter as she leaned against the building to watch the sun rise. It was a beautiful Montana morning; Jess only hoped tomorrow she would see it from behind the wheel of her car.

"HEY, HENRY! We're ready to roll!" Jess's cheerful voice penetrated through the motel room door and woke Henry from a light sleep.

"Coming!" There was no answer from Jess. Henry supposed she'd hurried off to pack the car again. They seemed to need to keep an amazing amount of paraphernalia with them; he'd watched from his seat in the restaurant as Jess and the children unloaded the station wagon and carted it all back up the stairs to their room. He'd felt guilty, too. He should have offered to help, but Jess was a woman who looked daggers at him whenever he offered a perfectly reasonable suggestion.

He looked at his watch, waiting a second for his eyes to focus. Three-thirty. Eddie the mechanic might be dependable, but he sure wasn't speedy. Henry eased himself off the bed, careful to avoid putting weight on his aching arm, and turned off the television set. He zipped up his bag and left the cool room, feeling the hot afternoon air hit his face as he stepped outside. It wasn't hard to spot the station wagon; the two kids were hanging out the windows and waving to him.

Jess stood at the tailgate rearranging boxes. Henry had to admit she was attractive, in denim shorts and a short yellow top that barely covered her waist. When she bent over to adjust the conglomeration of bags, pillows and boxes, a generous strip of satiny, tanned skin was exposed. Her long hair, pulled off her neck in some sort of goofy-looking ponytail, bounced as she worked. She turned to greet him, a smile on her face.

"We're all set," she said, looking pleased with herself.

He walked over to her and put his bag into an empty

space between rolled-up sleeping bags. "Eddie discovered what was wrong?"

"Let's hope so." She pushed the tailgate shut. "For now, this baby runs."

"Good." Henry didn't know what else to say. Jess looked as if she'd spent the afternoon beside the pool. She smelled fresh, like powder, and her skin was rosy. Her red nose didn't stand out as much as it had yesterday.

"Okay." She rolled up the window, and Henry walked around to his side of the car and got in. The vinyl seat was hot; he was glad he'd worn cotton slacks. His navy polo shirt was already beginning to feel sticky. Why had he gotten himself into this situation? Tonight he would call G.H. and tell him to count him out. He would fly home and heal in private.

Jess got in the car, and Henry tried to avoid looking at her legs. He turned around and looked at the children instead.

"Hi, Henry," Jeremy said. Sue, combing her wet hair, only smiled hesitantly.

"Hello." He never knew what to say to children.

Jess inserted the key into the ignition. "This feels like an instant replay," she said.

"You're obviously feeling better." Henry decided he was happier when she was puffy and unattractive.

"Antibiotics are amazing, don't you think?" The motor roared. Jess eased up on the gas and let the engine idle. "What about you? Are you feeling better?"

He nodded toward the ignition. "I am now."

She slid her sunglasses on, adjusted the rearview mirror and put the car in reverse. Soon they were out of the parking lot and shortly afterward veered onto Interstate 90. Henry picked up the map folded on the seat. He tipped it sideways to read the mileage chart. "Three hundred and forty-one miles to Billings."

"We'll have to go to Bozeman tonight, instead," Jess said. She turned on the radio with her right hand and fiddled with the dial until she found a station with music.

"Bozeman?" He checked the chart again. "That's only two hundred miles!"

She remained calm. "It's already four o'clock."

"At this rate, we'll be on the road for weeks."

"I don't like to drive at night." Jess turned up the volume on the radio and began to sing along. The highway was practically hers alone, the sun was at her back, and the air from the window cooled her heated skin. She glanced in the rearview mirror to see the children reading. They'd been swimming for hours and would be sleepy, so she was optimistic that there'd be very little noise from the back seat this afternoon. Henry could bitch all he wanted to, but Jess was determined to get another good night's sleep instead of driving half the night just to get to Billings to accommodate Henry Myles's schedule. He would have to learn to roll with the punches; he was much too inflexible.

Jess thought of telling him so, then looked over at him and lost her nerve. He'd put on his sunglasses and a magazine lay open on his lap. She concentrated on the road and thought about Henry's profile—straight forehead, long nose and strong chin. She sighed. She would have preferred a cheerful, elderly grandmother for a passenger, someone who liked to chat and called the children "little dears." Her second choice would have been a college student, who would have let the trip "happen" and liked loud music. Instead she was stuck with someone *stuffy*, who looked at her as if she was mold on his morning toast.

Jess kept their speed at fifty-five, cruising along the open highway past miles upon miles of fields. Rough-hewn homesteads and an occasional sawmill dotted the scenery.

"If that was any louder we'd be in a bar."

She lowered the radio's volume. "What?"

"My eardrums thank you."

"It's too loud?"

"That, and your singing along at a high-decibel level, too."

"Oh." So what was the big deal? Maybe his mood was contagious; she was starting to feel a bit cranky herself. "You have a problem with that?"

He turned to face her. She wished she could see his eyes, but the sunglasses hid them. "You seem to know a lot of country songs."

"I guess so. I never thought about it." Maybe four years of waitressing everyday in a café with a radio on could qualify her as a disk jockey, if nothing else.

"Is there anything else on besides country and western?"

"No, I don't think so, but you're welcome to try. This just has AM."

She thought he muttered something about the Dark Ages but she wasn't sure. The static hid his words as he turned the dial back and forth. Jess thought she recognized Conway Twitty and a few notes of the latest K.T. Oslin song before Henry tired of trying to locate a radio station to his taste. He found the station she'd been tuned in to and leaned back against the seat.

"I give up," he said.

"Smart of you."

"I should buy a Walkman at the next town."

Jess decided to be polite. "What kind of music do you like to listen to?"

"Jazz."

Jess sighed. That figured. He would like obscure music with no discernible tune. "No words?"

"No words." His tone was emphatic.

"I've never understood that. Don't you wish you could sing along?"

He was staring at her. She could feel his gaze so she turned to look at him before facing the shimmering concrete road ahead of her. "Well, don't you?"

His voice was cold. "It never occurred to me."

It was going to be a long afternoon, Jess decided. Maybe conversation would make the miles go by faster. "Why not?"

"Why do you think music has to have words?" he countered.

"To sing with."

"No." He shook his head. "The beauty is in the music."

"The poetry is in the lyrics."

"Poetry? 'The last time I saw Momma she was waitin' for a train'?"

"Very good! Now you're getting the hang of it." She laughed, not able to help herself. It was fun having someone to banter with. She raised her voice. "Jeremy, would you get me something cold to drink?"

"Sure, Mom," the boy said, and ducked down behind Henry. There was a squeak and the rustle of ice.

"What about you, Henry? Thirsty?"

Henry twisted around to look behind him. "You bought a cooler."

"Yep," she said proudly. "One of those inexpensive things. I bought ice and cans of soda pop and juices at a grocery store near the motel."

"Diet, Mom?" Jeremy held up a can for approval.

"Yep. Thanks."

Jeremy opened the can and put it into his mother's outstretched hand. "Can I have a root beer now?"

Sue called from the back, "Me, too?"

"Sure," Jess said. "Henry, do you want root beer, cola or orange juice?"

"Cola's fine," he said stiffly. "I'll pay for it—"

She shook her head. "Don't worry about it."

"I said I would pay for it." He took off his glasses and wiped his arm across his sweaty forehead, then shifted in the seat and rubbed the back of his neck.

Jess gritted her teeth. The man had a stubborn streak the size of the Rocky Mountains. "You can replace what you drink, okay?"

"Fine," he agreed, taking the can from Jeremy. "Thanks."

"Want me to write it down?" the boy asked.

"Please."

Jess rolled her eyes. *Help me, Lord, I'm traveling with a man who wouldn't know fun if it jumped in his lap.* Wrong analogy. A man who looked like Henry probably had women volunteering for lap duty. But what was Henry's idea of fun? She wondered if she should ask him. Not today, but there were a lot of miles and hours between here and New York. It might be an interesting conversation.

For now she was content just to drink the cold soda. She stuck the can between her legs when she wasn't drinking. She hoped Henry wouldn't think that was odd, but he didn't seem to notice. At least the can was out of the way of the steering wheel, and the cold metal felt good between her thighs. Jess turned the radio up higher and, recognizing the song, began to sing.

"WAIT HERE while we go get the rooms," Jess said to the kids. She parked the car under the light in front of the huge motel's registration office. "And lock the doors."

She got out of the car and stretched, then glanced at

her watch. It was after ten o'clock. The air felt cool and the dark black sky was full of stars.

"Are you coming?" Henry asked, already waiting on the steps.

Jess paused by the rear of the car. Her muscles tingled, and her right leg ached from pressing the gas pedal, but she felt good. Her head didn't ache and her nose wasn't running. Who could ask for more? "Have you ever seen such an enormous sky?"

"No." He shifted impatiently, his hand already on the office door.

"I haven't, either," she said.

"Look," he said, "after we get our rooms you can stand out here all night long if that's what really makes you happy, but I'm going inside now."

Jess waved to the kids, and followed Henry into the brightly lit office. They gave their names to the man behind the counter. Jess got her wallet while Henry tapped his credit card nervously on the counter. He looked exhausted, and as though he was in pain. It was no wonder he was anxious to take off that uncomfortable-looking sling and lie down with the weight of the cast off his neck.

The man punched numbers into the computer and then handed Henry a form to fill out. "Room 318, sir. Around the west side of the building, all the way to the back, third floor." Then he looked as Jess. "Would you spell your last name again, please, ma'am?"

Jess did, and the man turned back to the computer to punch in the name.

"How did you make this reservation, ma'am?"

"I called the 800 number."

"When?"

"About three hours ago, from Butte."

"We weren't able to hold your reservation, ma'am,

I'm sorry. Without a credit card number the room couldn't be held past nine o'clock."

"But I didn't want to charge it to my credit card."

"Whether you charge it or not, the credit card guarantees the room will be held for you no matter what time you arrive at your destination. It's after nine, ma'am, and because the college rodeo championships are being held here in Bozeman, the rooms are sold out." He looked so upset Jess was afraid he would cry. She knew she wanted to.

"Oh, dear," she said.

"I'm real sorry, ma'am. Whoever took the reservation should have explained all this to you."

Jess turned to Henry. "Well, that's that." She tucked her wallet back in her purse. "There are a bunch of other big motels around here. I'm going to make some calls and see if anybody has a room."

"Jess—"

"Don't say anything. I feel like an idiot." She went over to a row of pay phones and dug out the book of yellow pages. Henry finished signing for his room and took the key from the cashier. Then he waited by the phone for Jess to finish.

"Any luck?"

She shook her head. "Everything's full. The rodeo, they said."

"I thought the parking lot looked jammed."

"Me, too."

Henry rubbed the back of his neck and sighed. "You can have my room."

Jess was silent. There didn't seem to be any way out of this ridiculous situation, but she wished she could think of one. "We'll share it."

"That's what I meant."

"This is awkward."

"Don't worry about it."

Jess started to leave the motel lobby, but Henry turned back and spoke with the man at the desk, who nodded. Henry caught up with her by the glass doors. "I asked them to send up a cot."

"That's great. Thanks." She went outside, still embarrassed by the reservations fiasco. She'd thought everything was going so well, now that the car was fixed, and here she was spending the night with Henry. She knew she was lucky, though; she could have been sleeping in the parking lot, or driving until the next town, which in Montana meant a hell of a long way.

Jess drove around to the other wing of the motel, Henry sitting quietly beside her. The sleepy children were silent, listening to music through their headphones.

"Bozeman must be a pretty busy place," Jess whispered.

Henry nodded. "Montana State University is here. I saw it on the map."

Minutes later, after parking in a spot Jess was sure was illegal, she called the children to start unpacking the car. Everyone took something; Jess carried the bird cage and her suitcase, her large tote bag slung over her shoulder. Henry managed his own bag and led the way to the entrance. They followed him up the stairs to the third floor and down the hall, which had green indoor-outdoor carpet.

"I feel as if I'm in a bad parade," Jess said. "Don't you?"

Henry ignored her and stopped in front of one of the rooms.

"Where's our room?" Sue asked as Henry put down his bag and dug the room key out of his pocket.

"There was a mix-up with the reservations so we're all sharing this one," Jess said, trying to sound as if it would be fun.

"All of us? How are we gonna fit?" Jeremy asked.

"We'll manage," Henry said grimly.

The room was large, with two queen-size beds. The bedspreads were gold, the carpet forest green. Henry went over to the ventilation unit under the window and adjusted the dials. A fan roared to life. Jess hoped it would relieve the stuffiness.

"Could we open the window, too?" she suggested.

Henry pushed back the flowered drapes and checked. "No. It doesn't open."

Jess set the bird cage on the dresser and lifted the cover. "Good night, Harrigan." She waited for an answer, but the bird just blinked and tucked one leg in to his chest. Jess dropped the corner of the cover back over the cage and hoped it would be as easy to get her children into bed. Sue ran into the bathroom and shut the door, and Jeremy turned on the television set.

"Keep it quiet, will you, please?" Jess asked.

Henry stood awkwardly by the window. "We'll put the cot along the wall by the window. I'll sleep on it."

"Nonsense," Jess said. "Jeremy can take that. You take one of the beds. Sue will sleep with me. She did last night and it's no problem."

Jess began to unpack the bags. "When Susan comes out of the bathroom, go put your pajamas on and brush your teeth, Jeremy. It's late."

The boy yawned, and tried to hide it. "This is cable, Mom. There's a good movie on HBO. This guy is shooting people—"

"That's *Die Hard*," Henry said, coming closer to stand near Jeremy who was sitting on one of the beds. "It's pretty violent."

"It sounds awful," Jess said. "Turn if off, Jer." She handed him his bag.

"But it's a great movie," Henry said. "And it just started."

There was loud machine gunfire. "Wow!"

Too tired to argue, Jess gave up and turned to Susan as she came out of the bathroom. "Get your nightgown on, Susan, and brush your teeth."

"Can I sleep in this T-shirt?"

"Sure, why not? Just brush your teeth."

The cot was delivered and pushed against the wall, and although it took longer than Jess had envisioned, the children were soon settled in bed. The room lights were turned off and only the dim glow of the television screen lit the room. After a brief argument with her son, Jess turned the volume even lower.

Now it was her turn to get ready for bed. Henry sat on his bed in front of the television and Sue was tucked into the other one. Jess felt the weariness in her bones and wanted to take a long hot bath to rinse off the perspiration and the Montana dust. But she felt awkward, especially when it came to changing her clothes. She usually slept in an extra long T-shirt. No underpants. Tonight she would wear them, just in case she had to get up in the night. She hadn't packed a robe because she'd thrown her old ratty one in the dump, along with most of her old clothes.

"Henry, do you, uh, need to use the bathroom? I'm going to take a bath."

"No," he said, propping up the pillows on the bed and leaning back. He didn't even look at her. He and Jeremy were absorbed in the movie, so Jess picked up her things, went into the bathroom and shut the door.

Alone. It was heaven. She quietly locked the door—she didn't want Henry to think she thought he would burst in, yet she had only known the man for a day and a half and you couldn't be too careful. She hoped the kids wouldn't think they were all going to share a room every night. Jeremy and Henry seemed to have the same taste in movies, so the child most likely felt as if he had an ally.

Jess adjusted the faucets and stepped into the tub, letting the water reach almost to the top before she shut it off. She slid underneath the water, then shampooed her hair and rinsed. Leaning back against the cool porcelain, she closed her eyes.

The tapping woke her up.

"What?"

"Jess? How long are you going to be?"

"Oh," she said, struggling to sit up. "I must have fallen asleep. I'll be out in a minute.

There was silence from the other side of the door. Jess pulled the stopper and stood up, feeling refreshed. The bathroom felt like a sauna and the mirror was steamed over. She grabbed a thick white towel and dried herself, tossing a hand towel over her hair to catch the drips. She dusted baby powder on her body and put on the nightshirt, plus a clean pair of panties. After quickly rinsing out the tub, she brushed her teeth and took a comb to start fixing her hair. Then she opened the door to let the steam out and dried the mirror with a towel. She felt cheerful again.

Henry stood in the doorway. "You could have drowned." He'd removed his shirt and his chest was bare. It was a hard, strong chest and looked different without the sling covering it. She looked back up to his pale face; he was in pain again, she guessed.

"I was just dozing," Jess protested. She hoped he couldn't see through her shirt; she'd intended to jump into bed before he had a chance to look too closely. Not that she thought he'd really bother. "It's all yours," she said. "Just let me get my things."

"The children are finally asleep," he said.

"Is the movie over?"

He nodded, stepping away from the doorway to let

her pass, but she hurried out so fast she bumped into him anyway.

"Damn," he said.

"I'm sorry. I hit your arm, didn't I?"

"I shouldn't have taken it out of the sling, but my neck is rubbed raw by the damn thing."

"Let me see...I might have some cream for it."

"No, that's okay...."

"Really," she said, "let me look...." She rummaged through her tote bag on the bathroom floor and came up with a tube of ointment. "Good old zinc oxide. Sit on the, uh, toilet seat and I'll put some on your neck."

"I can do it," he grumbled.

"No, you can't. You can't even see it."

He did as he was told. Jess decided it might be one of the first times in his adult life that he'd obeyed an order. She wanted to laugh until she looked at the raw pink skin at the back of his neck. "Oh, Henry. This looks so sore." She smoothed the heavy white cream over the red area. "How does that feel?"

"Great." He sighed.

She let her fingertips move lightly over his neck, patting gently to cover the sore part. "What about the front?"

"It's fine," he said, but Jess didn't believe him. She moved around to check the front of his neck, under his chin. His lips were firm and smooth and looked incredibly soft, so she tried to ignore that part of his face and concentrate on the side of his neck.

Henry felt Jess's soft hair sweep across his bare shoulder. She was too close, he decided, as the sweet scent of her skin surrounded him. He peeked down, following the rosy blush on her cheeks to the delicate outline of her lips. Henry weakened. He caught her shoulder and firmly pressed her to him, kissing her on the lips with a sudden passion that surprised him.

After a few seconds, Jess overcame her shock and forced herself to pull away. The kiss had been warm and thrilling and entirely too magnetic. "What the hell do you think you're doing?"

He looked unperturbed. "Jess, when you lean in front of a man's face smelling the way you do, you shouldn't act so surprised if you get kissed."

"Well, I am surprised. I was just trying to fix the sore spot on your neck."

"Of course," he said, sounding as if he were trying not to laugh. "And it feels much better."

Jess felt her face flush and struggled to think of something to say to change the subject. "Do you have to use the sling all the time?"

"If I don't, my arm hangs down and throbs."

"Oh." She concentrated on replacing the cap on the tube of ointment. "There."

"Thank you."

She backed up and tossed the tube in the bag. "You're welcome."

"Wake me in the morning whenever you're ready to leave," Henry said.

"Fine." Jess left the bathroom and climbed into bed beside her daughter, nudging the child gently so she would have some room. Then Jess heard the bathroom door shut and water start running. Henry must be going to take a bath, too. He couldn't shower, she supposed, with a cast on. But he didn't have any trouble kissing. In fact, he'd been downright fantastic.

He couldn't be in all that much pain if he'd had the energy to make a pass at her. She would refuse to feel sorry for him any longer.

4

HENRY SILENTLY BERATED himself. *You're a stupid jerk, an idiot of the greatest proportions. A fool.* Kissing Jess, along with the stupid excuse about her rubbing cream on his neck and standing so close... What had gotten into him? When had the smell of baby powder on a woman become so alluring?

Henry could only blame it on his weakened condition, he decided; pain pills could have changed his brain chemistry, lowering his resistance to strange women. He'd just read an article in *Newsweek* about drugs and depression. He'd be sharing the tissue box with Jess next, if he wasn't careful. The arm didn't hurt as much now; he could probably get by on aspirin.

He made sure the bathroom door was locked before turning on the faucets. He didn't need sleepy children wandering in to join him. Henry stripped, being careful to fold his slacks. No telling when he'd have a chance to do laundry. This entire ridiculous situation was G.H.'s fault, and Henry longed to call the old man and tell him so.

But something didn't quite make sense. Jess didn't appear to be anything like G.H.'s Las Vegas love.

Henry carefully lowered himself into the hot water, making sure he kept his arm dry. Here he was, taking stupid baths. Sitting in your own dirt, that was all it was. When he returned to Seattle, when his cast was off and his life was back to normal, the first thing he was going to do was take a shower. A cold one.

JESS HAD TO WAKE Henry up, but she didn't know how to do it without touching him. His bare shoulders peeked from beneath the white sheet, and she could see that his broken arm was carefully positioned across his matted chest. The sheet covered the rest of his large body, thank goodness. Jess didn't think he was the kind of man who slept in the nude—she pictured him more as the paisley-pajama type. Still, she didn't want to startle him into jumping out of bed, no matter what he was, or wasn't, wearing. It probably wouldn't be a great start to the day, not as far as Henry was concerned.

She stepped closer. He was snoring softly; it was a comforting masculine sound Jess suddenly realized she'd missed. Part of her didn't have the heart to disturb him. But another part of her was determined to be on the road early this morning. She wanted a thermos of coffee, a box of doughnuts and a glorious Montana sunrise.

After she'd taken her turn in the bathroom, and dressed herself in khaki shorts and a white T-shirt, she tiptoed back into the room. She kissed Sue until the sleepy child finally opened her eyes and smiled.

"Time to get up," Jess said. "You can go back to sleep in the car if you want to."

Sue staggered to the bathroom while Jess tried to wake Jeremy. After both children were up and dressed, she turned back to Henry. There was still the problem of waking him. She could let the children do it, but she guessed he wouldn't appreciate it. Still, Jess thought, going closer to the bed, who cared what he appreciated?

"Henry," she tried.

Nothing happened. Jess studied his face. Why had she made such a big deal out of one little kiss? After all, there'd been no passionate intertwining of bodies—

just a simple kiss and a jolt of longing that shocked her into rethinking the wisdom of traveling with Henry Myles. She ordered herself to forget the kiss. Just because it was a long time since she'd kissed anyone more than ten years old didn't mean she had to dwell on it.

"Henry," Jess said loudly.

The rhythm of his breathing changed, and his arm moved a fraction of an inch. Jess figured she was making progress. "*Henry*, wake up. Time to hit the road."

His eyes opened and he looked directly at her, but Jess could tell he didn't know where he was. She watched as he focused on her face. He almost smiled, then stopped.

"All right," he said, his voice ragged. "It's still dark. What time is it?"

"Almost five."

Henry sighed and struggled to sit up. He didn't know how to get out of bed with her standing right there. He had jockey shorts on, but that was definitely not enough. The lack of privacy made him cross. Remembering kissing Jess last night made him feel even worse.

"Sue and I are going to start loading the car. Jeremy will be out of the bathroom in a minute."

"Fine," he said, his voice gruff. As soon as the door shut, Henry tossed the sheet aside and sat on the edge of the bed. He heard the toilet flush, then the bathroom door opened and a triangle of light brightened the room.

"Guess it's just us guys," Jeremy said.

"Guess so."

Jeremy picked Henry's slacks off the chair. "Here," he said, handing them to him.

"Thanks." It was awkward putting on his pants with only one good hand, but he managed. He left the belt unhooked and went into the bathroom. He shaved quickly and brushed his teeth. When he came out, Jess was back.

She picked up the bird cage, "We'll be in the car."

"I'll be right down."

"I double-checked to see if we left anything behind. It's just your things here now."

"Fine," Henry said. "I'll meet you at the car." Once she'd left, Henry gathered his things together, pulled the hated sling over his head and tucked his heavy cast inside. His neck felt better than it had last night, but it was still sore. The weight of the cast didn't help. He grimaced, zipped up his bag and looked around the room. He'd remember this place.

JESS STOPPED at a service station for gas and coffee before getting back on the interstate.

"How long until Livingston?" Henry poured himself another cup of coffee from the thermos.

"Twenty miles," Jess answered. She balanced the plastic cup on the dashboard and checked the speedometer. It felt as though they were going faster than fifty-five miles per hour on the empty stretch of highway. The children had gone back to sleep, lulled by the humming of the tires on the dark road. Dawn lightened the sky and the Gallatin valley, its miles of wide-open range country becoming visible. Jess was quiet, still feeling awkward about the unexpected physical contact with Henry last night.

Unable to stand the tension any longer, she pulled the car off to one side of the road.

"What's wrong?" Henry asked.

"Nothing." She turned off the engine and stepped out of the car.

"Where are you going?"

"I want to see the morning." Goose bumps rose on

her bare legs, and Jess was glad she'd put a sweatshirt on over her T-shirt.

Leaning against the side of the car, she watched the horizon turn shades of peach and pink. Rose streaks licked the broad expanse of sky, and the rising yellow sun highlighted scattered cloud wisps. Tears burned her eyes; it was more beautiful than she'd ever imagined. The earth warmed instantly as the sun flamed above the horizon. She blinked against its brightness and turned back to the car.

Henry stood propped against his open car door. "Quite an entrance. I hope it's not going to be another hot day."

"Is that all you can say?" She tossed him an exasperated look, then slid behind the wheel and shut her door. She waited for Henry to get settled, then started the car. The silence hung between them, but Jess didn't turn on the radio. She wanted to enjoy the peace and quiet of the morning and pretend she was all alone. Mercifully, Henry remained quiet. Jess hoped he'd decided to enjoy the beauty of the morning.

She turned off the interstate at the exit to Livingston. "I think we'd better stop here and eat breakfast," she told Henry. "It's more than two hundred miles to Billings and nothing in between."

"Fine," he said.

Jess spotted the familiar golden arches and pulled into the restaurant parking lot.

"Not again," Henry groaned.

"We agreed. I get to pick." She pulled off her sweatshirt and tossed it in the back seat.

"Are we going to eat every meal in these places?"

"It's cheap and good and the kids like it." That was the last word as far as Jess was concerned. Besides, she'd noticed that Henry never hesitated to order a huge amount of food.

They took their time eating, though Henry pointedly looked at his watch several times. Once on the road again, Jess knew it was going to be another hot day after all. The sun's rays soon warmed up the front seat of the car. The large expanse of windshield blasted heat onto the dashboard and into her face; the cool predawn air was a distant memory.

Three hours later, after passing Billings, Jess stopped at a gas station on the interstate.

"It's like traveling in hell," Henry muttered, staggering out of the car.

"It's a heat wave," Jess said, wiping perspiration from her forehead. "I don't think Montana is usually this hot." She tossed the water from the cooler onto the ground.

Jeremy's expression was pained. "I hafta go to the bathroom."

"Are we eating here?" Susan asked.

"No," Jess said. She looked over at Henry. "Let's go inside and buy food for a picnic and eat at Custer Battlefield."

"A picnic?" he echoed.

"I don't think there are any restaurants at the battlefield," she answered.

"It's too hot to eat. Let's go inside and argue about it." Henry was already heading across the parking area.

Jess checked to make sure the bird was out of the sun, then ushered the children out of the relentless sunshine into the large convenience-store section of the cement building. She was too hot to argue about anything.

After a longer time than Jess would have anticipated, they were back in the hot car. The kids made an attempt to color but started fighting, so she ordered them to split up. Jeremy took the back seat and played with G.I. Joe action figures while Susan spread her three Barbie dolls and their clothes in the back of the wagon. Jess attempted to drown out their bickering by turning on the radio.

Miles of waving yellow grass lined the sides of the highway as they drove across the prairie of eastern Montana. "It looks like something out of a John Wayne movie," she said.

Henry looked up from the map. "It's about fifty miles to Custer. Are you sure you want to stop?"

"It's history, Henry. When will we ever get to see a place like this again?"

Henry didn't care. Heat shimmered from the dashboard and into his face. "Let's just drive by and point. The kids won't mind."

"We have to eat lunch," Jess insisted. "Might as well do it there, where there's something to see."

Henry surveyed the landscape. There was nothing but prairie for miles in all directions. He leaned back, resting his aching head against the seat, and listened to Jess sing.

Jess followed the signs to the monument and veered off the highway and onto a two-lane paved road. She was glad she'd pulled her hair up in a ponytail at the last stop; perspiration soaked the back of her shirt and she was sure the seat of her shorts was wet. At least the shorts were light brown, the same color as Montana dust, and they were long enough so she didn't burn her thighs on the vinyl seat every time she got into the car.

They passed a large old building whose sign said Trading Post; then the road twisted and climbed up a hill to the visitors' center parking lot. Jess drove slowly through the lot, looking for a shaded place to park the car. She finally found one, in front of a green lawn that, according to the sign, was part of a national cemetery. Neat rows of white headstones lined the grass.

"Great," Jess said, turning off the engine. "We're in the shade."

Henry opened his eyes and sat up. "It's a tree."

"Yep," she agreed, opening the car door and looking over to the lawn. "It's a nice evergreen."

"And shade," he murmured, peeling his sweaty clothes from the vinyl seat.

"This is true," Jess agreed again, trying to humor him. She turned to the kids. "C'mon, guys, we're going to go see where General Custer met the Indians." The kids scrambled out of the car. Jess looked over to Henry. "Are you coming?"

"Sure," he said, wiping his brow, "as soon as the tree stops spinning."

"What?" Jess frowned. Henry's face was red and blotchy and he looked terrible. "Are you okay? Maybe you should go splash some water on your face."

"Good idea," he said, climbing slowly out of the car.

Jess locked the car, making sure the windows were rolled down an inch. "Will you take Jeremy to the men's room with you? I hate to have him go into these public places by himself."

"Sure." Henry nodded. "This is really hell." He glared at the station wagon as if it were a motorized torture chamber and slammed the door. "I can't believe how hot the inside of that car is."

"Think how the pioneers felt," Jess said, hoping to make him smile. He didn't. They walked along the sidewalk to the visitors' center. After she and Sue used the ladies' room, they peeked inside the museum, then waited near the outside entrance for Jeremy and Henry.

Henry didn't look any better. "I can't seem to cool off," he said. "And I have chills."

"Uh-oh. Heat stroke, Henry. I don't think you're doing very well." She hoped he wouldn't pass out. What would she do with an unconscious man? "Sue, run back to the bathroom and get a bunch of paper towels, please."

When Sue returned, Jess ordered Henry back to the car. She grabbed one of the sleeping bags from the back and spread it out in the shade of the little tree. "Lie down," she told him. He obeyed without question.

Jess knelt by his head and loosened the knot of the sling. Then she hauled the cooler out of the car and set it on the grass. "I think we need to lower your body temperature," she said, taking the towels from Susan and dipping them into the ice water inside the cooler. She laid them on Henry's forehead.

"I won't argue with that," he said. "That feels great." The ice water felt almost as great as her gentle fingertips stroking his hot skin. He felt grubby and dizzy, but wished he could pull Jess onto his chest and kiss her. Spots danced before his eyes so he closed them. The cool water dripped along his temples and into his hair. "I've died and gone to heaven," he said sighing.

"Actually, you're not far off."

"What?" Did she know something about heat stroke that he didn't?

She chuckled. "You're only a few feet from the cemetery."

"Can we walk up there?" Jeremy asked. Henry wondered what "up there" meant.

Then he heard Jess's voice, sounding a little worried. "Sue, do you want to go with us to see the monument? It's at the top of that hill—see the people on the sidewalk? That's where they're going."

"Uh-uh," the girl answered.

"Stay here with Henry, then, and keep cold paper

towels on his head," Jess said. "You looked flushed, too. Have some juice. Guard Henry—"

"Guard Henry?" the subject of the conversation interrupted. "From what?"

"Rattlesnakes," she said. "Didn't you see the signs saying to stay on the sidewalks and away from the prairie? This hot weather makes *them* look for shade, too."

Henry envisioned lying quietly on the sleeping bag, sharing his cool cloths with a slithering reptile. Sleeping with a snake, what a way to spend a vacation. He would put it on a postcard. *Dear G.H., Wish you were here, weather is fine, snakes everywhere.* There was no doubt in his mind that if there were a rattlesnake around, it would find George Henry Myles III. That was simply the way things had been shaping up over the past weeks.

"Do you want your sandwich now, honey?"

"Uh-uh," Sue said.

Henry felt someone smooth the sleeping bag and sit near his feet. There was clicking, and then the tinny sound of music. Rock music.

"Henry?" Jess removed the towels for a moment and then replaced them on his forehead. "I'm taking Jeremy up to the top of the hill to see where Custer fell. Sue's here with you."

"Fine."

"She's going to stay right here until I get back. Don't let her wander off."

"Fine. No problem." Where would a little girl want to go around here, anyway?

He felt Jess lean closer. "You're looking a bit better," she said. "Not as blotchy."

Great, Henry thought. He'd have to add that to the postcard. *Not as blotchy.*

"Come *on*, Mom," Jeremy said.

"Okay." Jess moved away. "Let me get a hat. You put your baseball cap on. One person with heat stroke is enough." Her voice grew softer. "Stay here, Sue. We won't be long. Then I'll take you inside the museum."

"Inside?" Henry echoed. "Is it air-conditioned?"

"Sort of, but there's a couple of hundred people milling around. I think it's just as nice out here in the shade, with this little breeze."

"Oh." His hopes for cool air faded. Then there was quiet. He heard footsteps crunch on the gravel walk, then nothing but Susan humming along with the music. Just like her mother, Henry thought. He started to feel better. He heard people slam car doors, engines start and snatches of conversation. Still, the place seemed subdued for a tourist attraction. The cemetery and the scattered prairie headstones probably added to the quiet atmosphere. Or else, Henry decided, it was just too damn hot to talk. Just before he dozed off, Henry heard his rattlesnake guard rummage through the cooler.

"STAY ON THE PATH!" Jess called, watching her son race along the sidewalk. His energy remained unaffected by the blazing noonday sun, while Jess trudged slowly up the hill and wished she were back in the shade with Henry. She'd been crazy to let him kiss her last night, she decided. She was only human, though, and he was the handsomest man she'd ever seen, except for Ronny, the man who delivered the Hostess products to the café. But Ronny usually had a wad of chewing tobacco in his cheek and spit on the pavement before pushing the cartload of snacks through the door.

Henry hadn't spit yet. Jess almost wished he would.

Except for being grumpy, he didn't seem to mind her frank comments. He appeared to be unflappable—she could say just about anything to him and he took it in stride while tossing in a few blunt remarks of his own. At first, she didn't want to antagonize him, but Henry didn't have any scruples about antagonizing her, so they'd hit a middle ground. Now they said whatever they wanted to, each figuring the other could deal with the honesty. Not bad for the third day.

The wind blew hot and steady at the top of the knoll, whipping the long grass into waves. Jess joined her son and read the words on the monument to him.

"I feel sad for the Indians and sad for the soldiers," he said.

"I know what you mean."

"It's kinda creepy up here," Jeremy said.

Jess suddenly felt very much alone, and didn't like it. "Want lunch?"

He shrugged. "Yeah. Is Henry gonna be okay?"

She put her arm around Jeremy's bony shoulders and hugged him to her. "Sure, he is. He just got too hot."

"Oh." He grinned. "Race you back to the car?"

"No way. We walk, or we'll look like Henry—all red and blotchy."

By the time Jess returned to the car, perspiration soaked her clothes and she longed for shade. Henry lay quiet on the sleeping bag, and Sue was humming along to her Bon Jovi tape. When Jess knelt near the bag, Henry sat up.

"Here," he said, handing her a wad of brown towels. "You look like you need them more than I do."

"Thanks," she said, and wiped her face. "How are you?"

"I'll live."

"You'd better," she replied, too aware of the way his green eyes sparkled at her and tiny laugh lines crinkled at the corners. She lay on her back on the bag, careful not to touch him. "Does anyone want lunch?"

"Yeah," said Jeremy.

"I guess so," Sue added.

"It's up to you, Jess."

She closed her eyes and didn't move. "Fine. Kids, you're in charge. Get the paper plates and the bag of food out of the car and bring them over here. The sandwiches are in the cooler."

"Here, Mom," Sue set a can of soda on her mother's stomach. "It's diet."

Jess closed her fingers around the cold can. "Wonderful."

"Did you see any rattlesnakes?"

Jess shook her head. "Not one."

"Me, either." The child sighed.

Jess struggled to sit up. "Jeremy, put Harrigan on the hood of the car so he can get some air."

Later, after finishing every cold drink and all of the sandwiches and cookies, they locked everything—including the bird—inside the car and spent a leisurely hour touring the museum. For the first time, Henry wasn't in a hurry to get back to the car. They lingered on the covered deck, listening to a speaker describe the entire battle of the Little Bighorn. "It's after two," Jess said, finally ushering everyone outside. "We need to make it to Casper tonight."

Henry fell in step with her. "How many miles?"

"Two hundred and fifty, I think." Perspiration dotted her forehead. She predicted it was going to be a long afternoon and an even longer evening.

Once in the car again, the children rearranged the sleeping bag in the back while Henry grabbed his camera and took a few pictures.

"Harrigan looks funny," Susan said. "He's holding his wings up."

Jess peered over the seat. It was a strange sight—the

little parakeet leaning forward and holding his wings out from his body.

"He's cooling himself off," Henry explained, looking through the opened window. Jess appeared to be worried, and he didn't blame her. He didn't see how the bird could survive this heat, but he kept quiet, remembering how angry Jess had been last time he'd questioned Harrigan's chances for survival.

"I hope it works," she muttered. "Let's hit the road."

"Let's stop at the trading post and get something cold to drink before we get back on the highway," Henry said, getting in the car. "I'll buy."

Jess drove out of the parking lot and down the hill. "I don't know, Henry. It's getting late, and we have such a long way to go."

"It's insane to travel in this heat," he insisted. "And I'll bet that place is air-conditioned. We could all use some cold air, don't you think?" He tried to sound practical, but he would have jumped out of a moving car to get inside an air-conditioned building right about now. He didn't tell Jess, though. She might just let him jump, especially since he'd come on like Mr. Macho Stud last night.

"You win," she said.

The kids cheered when Jess pulled into the dusty parking area and stopped in front of the hitching rail. There was no one else around so Jess didn't bother locking the car. She left the windows rolled down, for Harrigan, and followed Henry and the kids onto the rough wooden porch. The building looked like a relic from the Old West, but decorating the door was a sign: No Shirts, No Shoes, No Service.

Susan tugged on Jess's shirt. "Can we buy something?"

"We'll see," Jess answered. She'd have to look at the prices first. It was cruel to take children into a gift shop and tempt them with things they couldn't afford to buy.

They passed aisles of shelves lined with Western souvenirs, history books, posters, beaded jewelry and colorful Indian artwork as they followed the arrows to the restaurant. The air conditioner blasted cold air into the empty cafeteria-style room, making Jess shiver. Even the plastic chairs were cold. She loved it, especially when Henry, one-handed, delivered a tray of large drinks to the table.

"Here," he said, passing Jess a big waxed cup. "Diet."

"Thanks." She poked a straw through the plastic lid, crunching through the ice, and took a sip. This was heaven.

He handed the children theirs. "Root beer," he announced. Then he sat down across from Jess. "Thanks for taking care of me back there."

Jess didn't know what to say. The man was acting so unexpectedly charming. It was out of character. The heat, she thought suddenly, had affected his brain. "Uh, no problem." She wished he wouldn't smile at her that way.

The kids noisily drained their drinks. "Can we go look around?" Jeremy asked.

"Just a minute," Jess answered. "Let me finish."

"I'll go with them," Henry offered. "You take your time."

"Are you sure?" She wanted nothing more than to sit in the chilly, quiet room and chew ice.

"Sure." He stood and adjusted his sling. "Meet us in the gift shop when you're done."

"Don't let them touch anything," she called.

"Oh, Mom," Sue wailed. "We're not babies."

"You're right." She laughed. "But this isn't a toy store, so keep your hands in your pockets."

A few minutes later, after a quick trip to the ladies' room, Jess wandered into the gift shop. The children were standing beside Henry in front of the cash register. He replaced his wallet in his back pocket just as Jess walked up.

"Look what Henry bought me, Mom." Jeremy held up a necklace with a copper arrowhead dangling from the chain. "Neat, huh?"

"Very neat," Jess agreed, wondering what was going on here.

"I got a bracelet," Sue said, proudly holding out her wrist where an inexpensive copper band gleamed.

"That's beautiful," Jess said. She turned to Henry. "You didn't have—"

"I know," he interrupted. "But I wanted to say thanks to my nurse and helper. It's been a tough few hours and they never complained." He handed her a flat bag. "I got some postcards for us."

Jess was touched by his thoughtfulness. "That's really nice, but you didn't have to—"

"I didn't *have* to do anything. I wanted to." He frowned at her, as if daring her to argue, then took the change the Indian woman handed him.

Deciding it was a good time to change the subject, Jess asked. "Are you going to write to G.H.?"

He nodded. "Are you?"

"I'll send him a postcard. He might like to know we've made it this far."

"I'll call him tonight. Any message from you?"

"No," she said, turning and heading for the door. "Just say hello from us."

Jess hesitated at the door, unwilling to leave the trading post and climb into the hot car. "Guess this is it," she said with a sigh. "Come on, kids."

"Guess so," Henry said. He wondered if he'd survive the next hundred miles.

The car was hot, the parakeet was still alive, and miles of prairie surrounded the highway.

Henry put on his sunglasses and picked up the map. "Where are we going?"

"Casper, Wyoming."

Jeremy poked his head over the seat. "How many miles, Mom?"

"You don't want to know."

"Then how many hours?" he persisted.

Henry answered for her. "Five or six, depending."

Jess glanced over at him. "Depending on what?"

"How many stops we make." He opened the road atlas to the page that showed Wyoming and handed it to Jeremy. "A new state."

"Wow!"

A new state. The thought made Jess's throat tighten. She was getting farther away from home all the time.

5

"I'M BORED."

"Me, too."

Me, too. Henry was asleep, so Jess didn't have the radio on. She was stuck with her own thoughts, which were definitely not entertaining. "Color," she suggested to the children. "You had fun doing that this morning, didn't you?" She watched in the rearview mirror as the kids scrambled to the back of the wagon and rustled through the boxes and pillows.

"Uh-oh," Jeremy said.

"What do you mean, 'Uh-oh'?"

Silence was her answer. Jeremy held up Henry's duffel bag for his mother to see. Blotches of blues, reds and purples decorated the nylon bag, the remnants of crayons that couldn't take the heat.

"You didn't put the crayons back in their box, did you?"

"Not really," Sue answered.

"Get some tissues and see if you can wipe it off." Even as she said it, she knew it was hopeless.

"Wipe what off?" Henry mumbled, sitting up straight. He took off his sunglasses and rubbed his eyes.

"Your bag," Jess said. "It's had an accident." So much for short-lived harmony.

Henry turned around to see. He swore under his breath.

"Do you want me to stop so you can clean it up?"

He shook his head. "Forget it."

Jess called to the kids, "Put the rest of the crayons in the cooler. If you want to color, dry them off but make sure you put them back when you're done."

"We're sorry, Henry," Sue called. "But it looks kinda pretty."

"I thought we'd stop in Sheridan to get gas and fill up the cooler."

"And make reservations for tonight in Casper," he added.

"Okay."

"Unless you want to spend another night together."

There was laughter in his voice, so Jess kept her eyes on the road in front of her. "Not tonight, dear, I have a headache."

He chuckled. After a few miles passed, he said, "Not much to see, is there?"

"I love it. There's something about the plains that makes me feel free—" She stopped. What made her think Henry would understand? She glanced over at him.

Henry studied the landscape, a thoughtful look on his face. "I don't think I could live here."

"Didn't you ever dream of being a cowboy when you were a kid?"

"No." Then he smiled. "A fireman. What about you?"

"You'll laugh."

"I promise I won't."

"I dreamed of being Miss America." She shrugged, a wry smile on her face. "I wanted to grow up to be tall and have long legs and wear lots of rhinestone jewelry."

"Did you ever get the rhinestones?"

"Very funny."

A few minutes of comfortable silence passed. "I used

to go out with a former Miss Washington," Henry offered.

"I'm impressed."

"She expected me to be, too."

Jess guessed from his tone that he hadn't been. She waited for him to say something more, but he remained quiet. When she grew tired of the silence, she switched on the radio and sang along as the miles rolled by. They were heading southeast now, so the sun wasn't directly in her face.

"Don't you have any family?" It was an abrupt question, but Jess was growing accustomed to Henry's idea of conversation. She stopped singing and turned the radio down.

"I was an only child," she said. "My mother died when I was seven, and my father was a sawyer for a big logging outfit. We moved around the Northwest a lot."

"That's how you ended up in Sandpoint?"

"Yep. My father took sick, one of those lethal kinds of cancer that takes hold and won't let go. He died right after I graduated from high school."

Henry realized how similar their childhoods were: a mother's early death, raised by a father who did the job right. But the similarities ended there. He'd had a solid family base, with no worries financially. "How did you live after that?"

"I moved in with a girlfriend, got a scholarship to North Idaho Junior College for a year. Then I worked. I met my husband—who was in the logging business, too—and that was that."

Until G.H.? Henry wondered. Now for the sixty-four-thousand-dollar question. "How did you meet my grandfather?"

"At the café where I worked as a waitress, remember? Didn't he tell you?"

"I don't remember," he lied.

"He's a real charmer, isn't he?"

He stopped himself from shuddering. "He sure is." He decided talking about G.H. was not the best idea in the world. Henry understood how his grandfather could have fallen for Jess's vulnerability—she looked fragile, but was so damned independent and cheerful. He didn't blame the man who'd say, "Let me take you away from all this." *He* wouldn't be caught dead uttering those words, but he was beginning to understand why a man would be tempted to. And why G.H. had manipulated him—broken arm and all—into this old car to "protect" this family. He looked at Jess. Singing again. She knew the words to every song on the radio and hadn't missed a note in three days. "Were you a music major?"

"What?"

"Were you a music major in college?"

"No. Business administration."

It didn't fit. He would have guessed nursing. Or teaching. But then he remembered why she was moving. "Real estate?"

"No. I just got interested in that a few years ago. I thought it looked like a business a woman could do well in, without the corporate ladder stuff. I thought in real estate I could make my own hours and eventually have my own business."

Henry didn't bother to ask why she hadn't tried selling houses in Idaho. The economic problems there were no secret. "But you'll be working on commission."

She sighed. "I know. I have interviews with real estate companies. I know it's not an easy business, but there are plenty of jobs in New England, the kind that put food on the table, and I've saved some money. There's a little rent money coming in from my home in

Idaho, and enough insurance money left to stake us for a while."

"Sounds like you have it all figured out," Henry said. There'd been no mention of any other income, not that she'd say anything to her boyfriend's grandson, but no one could accuse this woman of extravagant spending. He hated to admit he could have been wrong about her, but he didn't want to make a hasty decision. After all, he fumed, he was in the car with her whether or not she was Miss Goody Two-shoes.

"I DON'T KNOW how to tell you this," Henry began, wondering whether to laugh or be angry.

Jess looked over at him. "Tell me what?"

Henry lowered his voice. "Your daughter—" he allowed a chuckle to escape before he continued "—your daughter is shaving her legs with my manicure scissors."

"What?" Jess twisted the rearview mirror so that she could see into the back seat. Sure enough, Sue sat with her feet propped up, carefully snipping the hair off her legs.

"We should be grateful, I suppose," Henry said.

"For what?"

"That she selected the scissors and not the razor."

Jess gave Sue a lecture about respecting people's belongings, and the child looked abashed.

"Sorry, Henry," she whispered.

"No problem," Henry said. At least the incident had made a few more miles go by quickly.

"This isn't the end of this," Jess promised her daughter. "You know better than to touch things without permission."

"Jeremy dared me to do it," Sue explained.

"Yeah, right, get me into trouble, too," her brother grumbled.

"Quiet," Jess ordered. "Be quiet for the rest of the day."

SHERIDAN, WYOMING was situated on the plains before the Bighorn mountain range. Jess wished she were driving up into those huge rounded mountains instead of being parked outside a supermarket before heading south to another town. These might be the last mountains she'd see for years, she thought, staring into the distance.

"Mom!" Jeremy called through the opened back door. "I don't think Harrigan looks too good."

Jess's throat tightened. "What do you mean, Jer?" She poked her head into the car.

"He's holding his wings out again."

Jess knelt on the back seat, setting the bag of ice beside her. She peered toward the cage. "Let me see."

Jeremy lifted the cage. "See?"

"Hello, baby," Jess crooned to the little parakeet. "Hang in there, will you?"

Henry, carrying a paper sack full of soda cans, came up to the car. "You want these drinks in on top of the ice or underneath?"

"Just a minute," Jess said. "Harrigan's trying to cool himself off and it's not working."

"The sign on that building over there says 103 degrees, but I'll bet it's a lot hotter than that in the car."

"Thanks for sharing that with me," she answered. "I feel a whole lot better now."

Henry sighed. "I don't think birds have a very efficient cooling system, not in this kind of heat."

"There you go, acting like a bird expert again."

"I just said—"

"Never mind." Jess glared at him. "Up until now, that bird's done better in this heat wave than you have."

"Damn it, Jess." Henry set the bag of soda on the cement and reached inside the car for the cooler. "The ice is melting while we're standing here."

"Well, fix it. I have to think."

He shot a quick look at her face. Was Jess going to cry over that bird? Henry grabbed the bag of ice and dumped it in the cooler, then shoved the drinks inside. He almost felt sorry for her.

"What did the pioneers do in this heat?" he asked, hoping she'd answer and get her mind off Harrigan's imminent death.

"Beats me," Jess said, her voice ragged. "They threw a lot of stuff out on the trail to lighten the load." There was an assessing look in her eyes when she turned to Henry.

"Don't get any ideas," he said, replacing the lid on the cooler. "I'm not going anywhere."

She sighed. "I don't know what the settlers did. I think they either found water holes or died."

"Guess I'd better give this some thought." He gestured to the kids. "Come on, you two. I'm going to need some help."

"Where are you going?"

"Back inside the store. Just stay here in the shade with Harrigan until we get back. It won't take long."

He liked giving orders, Jess decided, slumping against the back seat. She'd let him get away with it this once, just because she was so tired. Not wanting to look at the poor bird, she closed her eyes until she heard the children's voices.

Henry was looking pleased with himself when he returned to the car. Jeremy and Sue each carried plastic bags and he held a stack of yellow plastic dishpans. "Air-conditioning," he announced. "The old-fashioned way."

"I don't get it," she said, getting out of the car.

"Here." He handed her the dishpans. "Separate these, then we'll put a block of ice in each one."

"And?"

"Quit looking at me as if I'd been out in the sun too long. Don't you get it? We're making cold air."

"We are?" She put the dishpans on the ground and watched as Henry instructed the children to unwrap the blocks of ice and put them in the pans.

"In theory, this should work," Henry told her. His smile was surprisingly kind. "The bird might like the cool air the melting ice will give off. As long as the water doesn't spill, it's an easy cooling system. It's cheap enough, too." The kids took two of the pans in the back of the wagon and placed them on either side of the bird cage.

Jess wished she'd thought of it first. "How much did it cost? I want to pay my share."

Henry started to argue, but recognized the stubborn tilt to Jess's chin. He named the cost, unwilling to stand in a hot parking lot and battle over a few dollars.

"Fine," Jess said. "You kids make sure Harrigan has plenty of water in his dish, and keep an eye on him." She placed the third dishpan beside her on the front seat and slid behind the wheel. Then she dug money from her wallet and handed it to Henry. He took it silently and tossed it in the glove compartment while Jess started the car and drove back onto the interstate.

"I made reservations in Casper tonight," Henry said.

"Two rooms, right?"

"What do you think?" He grinned at her. "You snore."

"I do not."

"Sure you do, like a freight train." Actually she didn't but Henry wanted to cheer up Jess by giving her a chance to argue with him.

"Harrigan's drinking!" Jeremy called.

"Great," Jess said sighing.

"He stopped holding his feathers—oops, there he goes again."

"Sing to him," Jess suggested.

"Isn't it supposed to be the other way around?" Henry asked as the children started singing a rousing chorus of "Harrigan."

"It's an old George M. Cohan song," Jess explained. "We're big *Yankee Doodle Dandy* fans. Have you ever seen that movie?"

"A hundred years ago."

"We know all of the songs."

No kidding. "I suppose the bird does, too?"

"Well—" she smiled at him "—if you sing a song with his name in it, he does somersaults on the perch. Maybe the song will cheer him up."

"At the risk of sounding like an ornithologist, wouldn't flipping around on his perch cause him to overheat?"

Her stricken expression told Henry that she wasn't going to argue. "Stop singing!" she yelled. "It might be too much for Harrigan to exercise!"

"He only did it three times," Sue said.

"Well, talk to him quietly and let him know you're right there with him. He's out of the sun, right?"

"Yeah," Jeremy said. "This ice is neat. Can we lick it?"

"Sure, why not?"

Henry turned to watch. They looked like deer at a salt lick. Not that he'd ever seen deer at a salt lick, but this was what he figured they would look like—semi-disgusting but getting the job done. He turned back to Jess. Her cheeks were pink, her bangs damp with perspiration.

"Do you want something to drink?"

She shook her had. "I'll wait," she said. "How's your arm doing?"

"Better. Most of the pain is gone."

"You seem, uh, better."

"Yes," he agreed, realizing suddenly that he meant it. "I'm getting better all the time."

"SHE THOUGHT I SAID cantaloupe and I said antelope...." Jeremy's voice faded into another giggling fit. "I can't believe it!"

"I can't believe we're still hearing about it," Jess muttered. It was dark when they entered Casper, and Jess was having a hard time finding the motel. Highway repairs and the detours around the construction complicated the process.

"It's the funniest thing I've ever heard in my whole life."

"We know," Henry said. "We get the picture."

"Ow! She hit me!" Jeremy yelled. "Can't you take a joke?"

"Both of you, stop it!" Jess had had it with being a mother. She was tired, and the children hadn't stopped bickering for 150 miles. She hadn't figured out how yet, but she knew she and Henry were not going to spend the rest of the trip listening to cranky children tease each other.

"Turn right," Henry said. "I can see the sign."

Fifteen minutes later, they had registered and were busy unloading the car. Jess winced when she handed Henry his bag, the melted crayons glopped over the top and sides. He took it gingerly, as if the wax were still dripping, but he didn't say a word. Jeremy, in a fit of giggles, tried to hide behind his mother.

"March," Jess snapped, tired of her son's silliness. He smirked, grabbed his Walkman and his bag and high-stepped into the parking area.

"Sue, you take my bag, too. I'll get the bird cage." Jess locked the car and, with Henry and the kids surrounding her, headed toward the lighted doorway of C wing, the northern part of the enormous three-story motel complex.

"We can't go swimming?" Sue moaned.

"Quit whining." The trek across the huge parking lot seemed to take forever, and the children continued to bicker. Jess wanted to lie down on the pavement and hope one of the luxurious-looking motor homes would run over her in the morning. She wondered why people stayed in motels when they owned RVs. She would gladly have hijacked the thirty-foot Winnebago parked beside her Chevy. She envied Henry. He could lock himself into his quiet motel room and enjoy total privacy. He wouldn't have to censor the television programs or make anyone take a bath.

"Pig!" Jeremy screamed. "You got me in trouble when you cut your stupid hairy legs!"

"Am not!" Sue returned. "It was your idea."

"Jeremy." Jess looked over to her son and continued walking. She kept her voice low. "Don't call your sister names like that."

"She hid my Bon Jovi tape in the car and it's gonna melt and I hate her cuz she *is* a dirty, rotten pig."

"Stop right now." She wanted to grab him, but holding the bird cage hindered her. "Keep your mouth shut, young man, and don't say another word until we get to the room or you'll get a spanking."

"You *said* we were going swimming," Sue grumbled.

Jess stopped again, and Henry crashed into her. She could feel the thud of his duffel bag against her backside.

"Sorry," he murmured.

Jess paid no attention to the laughter in his voice. She

concentrated on the little girl in front of her. "Young lady, it's nighttime. It's dark. There are stars out. I don't see a pool anywhere around here, and I don't care. We're not staying up late again tonight and we're not—I repeat, *not*—going to talk about swimming anymore. Got it?"

Sue sighed. "I guess so."

"Good. You and I still need to have a talk about this afternoon."

Jess straightened and headed toward the entrance. She longed for a friend to talk to. Where would Gayle be tonight? Monday was the steak and fries special at the café, and Gayle and John usually took the kids there for dinner. They'd be home by now, sitting on their deck drinking wine and enjoying the mountain breeze.

Once inside the doorway, the group of travellers straggled up a flight of stairs and through another door to a long corridor. "Left," Henry said, and walked silently beside Jess.

She tried to keep the bird cage balanced and Sue's old baby blanket from slipping off it, so the bright lights wouldn't upset Harrigan. *I've lost my mind,* she thought. *I'm moving across the country with two cranky kids and a stranger with heat stroke, I don't know where I'm going, I don't have a job when I get there, and I'm worried about upsetting a parakeet? I should have myself locked up.*

"Over here," Henry said, pointing to a door. "That's yours, and I'm two doors down across the hall."

"Great." She reached into her pocket for the key, thankful at least for Henry. He'd been so nice this afternoon, asking her questions about herself and even teasing about last night. Maybe they could both forget that kiss, that silly mistaken moment in the glare of the motel bathroom.

"Creep!"

"Pig!"

"That's it," Jess hissed, unlocking the door. "Get in the room—*now.*"

"I think this is my cue to leave," Henry said over Jess's shoulder.

"Good night," she said with a sigh. Why did she hate the thought of his leaving?

"Good night, Jess. Call me in the morning when you get up."

"Okay." Jess stood in the hallway and watched Henry walk to his room before she went inside to spank her children. There was no way she was going to put up with their bickering for another 2500 miles—or however long the trip turned out to be. She faced Jeremy and Sue. Their expressions were serious. "Should I spank you for this behavior?" she asked.

They solemnly shook their heads.

"One swat each, then showers. And from now on, if you want to be miserable and rotten to each other, save it for next month. I can't take it on this trip."

Half an hour later the children, tucked into separate beds, were watching television. The movie starred Chevy Chase, who was moving to the country. The kids lay giggling and Jess wished she could join them. She even wished she were in Vermont with Chevy Chase.

A gentle tapping on the motel door surprised her. "Who is it?"

"Henry."

"Oh." Jess opened the door and saw Henry standing in front of her. He'd changed into a royal-blue polo shirt, which looked devastating against his tanned skin. He wore clay-colored slacks and his hair was damp. "Are you going somewhere?" she asked.

"I took a shower."

Jess immediately felt grubby. She still had Custer

Battlefield dirt on her skin. "How do you take a shower with a broken arm?"

He smiled. "Slowly."

"How do you wash your hair?"

"I found a plastic laundry bag in the bathroom and put it over my cast." He tapped the dry plaster. "It worked, see?"

She opened the door wider and stepped back. "Come on in."

Henry hesitated and then stepped inside. He looked over at the children. "They seem to be in a better frame of mind."

"They were spanked, I'm afraid."

He shrugged. "They needed it. Don't beat yourself up over it."

"I should be more understanding. After all, they're stuck in a car for hours and hours—"

"You're only human," Henry said, touching her shoulder in a brief gesture of comfort. "And a pretty nice one, too."

She smiled up at him. "Is that a compliment?"

He nodded. "It's a dinner invitation. Want to join me?"

"What?" She looked at her watch. "It's after nine-thirty."

"And I'm hungry. We ate at six, remember? And I was still too hot then to enjoy the food."

Jess remembered Henry had drunk about a gallon of iced tea. "But the kids—"

"Will be fine," he finished for her. "They are exactly where they should be. And they probably need some time away from you as much as you need time away from them. There's a restaurant right across the street. We'll walk over there. If you're not hungry you can watch me eat a steak, and you can have whatever you want. Dinner, dessert, coffee, what do you say?"

"You want company?" Jess didn't believe that for a minute. "I should think you'd be happy to be alone for a change."

Henry shrugged. "I was lonely."

She laughed. "You're full of baloney. You just want me along to cut your steak for you."

"Oh, I don't know," he murmured. "I might want more than that."

Jess held his steady gaze for a long moment before looking away. "I don't look as good as you do."

"You're fine."

Fine? No one would ever accuse this man of gushing. "Okay," she said, attempting to smooth the wrinkles out of her baggy shorts. "I'll keep you company."

The restaurant was nicer—and darker—than Jess had expected. Once they were seated in a secluded corner booth, she stopped worrying about how she looked. "I hope the kids don't let anyone in."

"You told them not to seven times. I think they got the message." Henry casually studied the menu and tossed it aside when the waiter approached the table. "Are you sure you don't want anything, Jess? I'm buying." He smiled at her. "It's our first date."

It was his smile that disarmed her into thinking he was teasing. "First date!" she scoffed. He had more of a sense of humor than she'd thought. "Okay, I'll have the shrimp cocktail and a glass of white wine."

"The largest steak you have," he told the waiter. "Medium rare."

Jess enjoyed the shrimp and sipped her wine while Henry demolished an enormous platter of steak—which the waiter served, as Henry had ordered, cut into bite size pieces—and potatoes.

"So," he said, finally pushing his plate to one side, "where are we going tomorrow?"

"Nebraska."

"And tomorrow night?"

She smiled. "It's a big state. We'll have to see how far we get." It wasn't exactly the truth, but Jess didn't want to ruin the evening with an argument. "Have you ever heard of Fort Laramie?"

"I don't even know what it is."

"A real fort and an old Army barracks from the Indian-fighting days. Wouldn't it be fun to see? It's right on the way."

"Right on the way," he repeated. "Why don't I believe you?"

"Don't worry," Jess assured him, "You'll enjoy learning more Western history."

He grimaced. "I had enough today, thanks."

"How could you? You were passed out on a sleeping bag."

"Don't remind me." He signalled the waiter, then turned to Jess. "Let's order dessert."

Jess hesitated. "I don't know, Henry. We've been gone an hour and I should probably get back."

He shook his head. "You can take an extra twenty minutes for cheesecake and coffee. The movie after that Chevy Chase thing is another silly comedy about a teenager getting his driver's license. The kids will love it."

"Okay." Jess was too tired to argue. She felt as if she'd been dragged behind the car all day instead of driving it.

LATER, WHEN SHE and Henry walked along the motel corridor, Jess yawned. "I'll probably dream about battlefields tonight." She moved toward her door and pulled the room key from her pocket. "Thanks again for the meal, Henry. I really enjoyed it."

He stood close to her. "I thought you could use some cheering up."

"You were right." She smiled up at him. "I hate it when the kids fight."

"I don't think Sue will get into my duffel bag again." He smiled. "And the bird? How is he tonight?"

"He seems fine." Henry was standing disturbingly close. "I know it's silly to be attached to a parakeet, but he's awfully special to—"

"Come here," he said, holding out his good arm. Jess took a step forward, at the same time wondering why she so readily obeyed, and stepped into the comforting embrace of his arm. She tried not to touch his cast, but the plaster bumped against her breasts in a surprisingly erotic way.

"What are we doing?" she whispered.

"I'm kissing you good-night." His lips found hers as she lifted her head to protest the odd embrace. Henry's mouth silenced her, and he pulled her closer to deepen the kiss.

Jess slipped her arms around his neck to tangle in his soft hair and closed her eyes. His lips were warm, and the sweet probing of his tongue against hers made her feel as if she were melting. He tasted wonderful—hot and sweet—and he slowly caressed her spine through the thin cotton fabric until she thought she'd die from sheer pleasure.

Henry slowly released her mouth. Jess took a deep, shuddering breath, and looked up into those unfathomable green eyes. What was she doing? How could she be standing in the hall of a motel kissing a man she'd only met three days ago? She slid her hands from his neck and stepped back from the embrace.

"Good night," she murmured, turning toward the door.

"Wait," he said, his voice low. "You dropped the key." He picked it up and tucked it into her hand as she faced him again. Touching her chin, he placed a brief kiss on her lips. "Sleep well."

Sleep well? Easy for him to say, Jess decided, after stepping into her room. The children were sound asleep in front of the television, and Jess walked over to turn it off before opening her tote bag. She wanted to crawl into bed and pull the covers over her head. Sleep would be the only way she'd forget the last few minutes.

6

HENRY STEPPED into his pants and opened the door. Jess stood there looking beautiful...and frantic. It seemed natural to lean down and kiss her good-morning. He could feel her surprise and the flare of response she tried to hide.

"We're running late," she said.

"We are?" Her lips were full and soft. Henry played with the idea of kissing her again.

Jess frowned. "Don't do that."

"Do what?"

"Look at me like that." She put her hands on her hips. "I overslept."

"So did I."

"I guessed." She looked pointedly at his bare chest.

"Come on in," Henry said, still a little groggy. "You woke me up when you knocked." In his rush to answer the door, he hadn't had time to zip his fly. Zippers were tricky to manage with one hand, and he couldn't rush without risking harm.

Jess didn't look thrilled, but she entered the room. "It's after eight. We really need to get on the road."

"Do we have to hurry today?"

She stared at him in surprise. "I thought you were the one anxious to get this trip over with."

"I was. I am." Henry wrestled with the zipper, hoping it was a subtle struggle. Jess glanced at his crotch and looked away, pretending great interest in the flower painting over the bed. He laughed. There was certainly no dignity left now. "I don't suppose you'd offer to help me with this?"

Jess smiled at him, but her cheeks turned pink. "Don't even think it. Why don't you just put a shirt on to cover your, uh..." She gave up. "Until I leave."

"My 'uh'?" Henry sat on the bed and placed a pillow across his lap. "There. Better?"

"You have a great mind for problem solving."

"You mean my pillow?" He chuckled.

"Your ice in the pans. We need to stop and get more ice, plus stuff for lunch before we get back on the road."

Henry shook his head. "No more picnic lunches."

"What are you talking about?" Jess perched carefully on the edge of the bed.

"No more sandwiches, no drinks from a can at lunchtime, no picnics. Crushed ice—in waxed cups, maybe—would be nice, but air-conditioned restaurants are the only way the two of us are going to survive this heat."

She turned thoughtful brown eyes on him. He could almost see her calculating expenses. "I suppose," she said after a pause. "At least until we hit cooler weather."

"We're heading into Nebraska, Jess."

"Fast-food places are air-conditioned."

He should have known she wouldn't give up easily. "I've agreed to eat breakfast out of plastic boxes on a brown plastic tray, but that's all. Once a day is my limit."

"Are you always this bossy in the morning?"

Bossy wasn't the word Henry would have used for the way he felt this morning, especially with Jess sitting near him in the dim light of the room. "Not always," he said.

She hopped off the bed. "It's like a morgue in here,"

she said, walking to the window and pulling open the drapes. Henry blinked, adjusting to the bright light that spilled into the room. Beyond the parking lot, the plains stretched toward the enormous blue sky. It looked hot already. "There's a McDonald's down there," Jess said. "We could eat before we get back on the highway."

"All right," Henry agreed. "I need coffee." He needed Jess. Despite those baggy shorts she wore, he was painfully aware of the tantalizing curves beneath. She had a way of moving that drove a man to think of other things besides drinking coffee.... He wondered if perhaps he'd inherited his grandfather's eye for the ladies after all, the way he was lusting after a stranger in a motel room in—he had to think for a second—Casper, Wyoming.

"We need some air," Jess stated, poking at the buttons on the unit under the window.

Sounded like one of those country songs Jess was so fond of, Henry mused. I was *lust*-ing in *Cas*-per Wy-*o*-ing this *morn*-ing—

Jess turned and interrupted his thoughts. "What day is it?"

"Tuesday. Why?" How could he work the word *Tuesday* into his song?

She shrugged and walked away from the window. "I'm trying to pry the kids away from the television and start packing up the car. How long will you need to get ready?"

Henry didn't want to get ready. He wanted to close the curtains and pull Jess down on the rumpled bed and make love to her. He wanted to feel her thick blond hair slip over his skin. "Ten minutes," he said with a sigh.

"I'll meet you at the car."

"Fine." She left, shutting the door firmly behind her. Henry threw the pillow across the room.

"WAIT A MINUTE," Henry said. "I forgot something."

Jess, ready to push the shopping cart through the checkout, stopped short. She couldn't figure out how she'd been conned into roaming around a giant discount store when she should have been driving down the highway instead. Henry had claimed he needed to buy a few things, and Jess had to admit, she wanted to avoid climbing into the hot car as long as she could. The front seat would be hell again this morning.

She checked the time. Ten o'clock. They really should have been on the road long before now. She'd considered traveling at night to avoid the heat, but that would have ruined her plans for today.

Sue held up a bag of miniature chocolate bars. "Can we get these?"

"Get real," Jess said. The candy would melt in fifteen seconds and take forever to clean up. "We have juice, soda and cookies. That should be enough."

Sue made a face and turned to her brother. "It was worth a try."

Henry met them in the aisle. He looked pleased with himself as he held up several rectangular packages. "No more crayons," he announced.

He was acting so nice that it made Jess nervous. She wasn't certain whether this was the real Henry Myles or he was putting on an act. "So, what is it?"

"Modeling clay." He grinned at Jess. "Clean, easy to use, no mess."

"Brilliant."

"Thank you."

Jess wished she'd thought of it herself. "Throw it in the cart and we'll get out of here."

"I'm buying."

"No," Jess said. "You shouldn't be buying the kids presents."

"Why not? It's self-defense."

She stepped closer to him and whispered, "You're...between jobs."

Henry stared down at Jess, trying to figure out what she was talking about. Then he remembered the lie he'd told her. "My finances are not your problem." His tone was colder than he'd intended.

Her lips made a straight line before she said, "Of course not. I just don't think you should be spending—"

"Not another word," Henry said, gripping the boxes of clay. "I'm going over there—" he pointed to a stack of plastic foam coolers "—to buy a cooler for the children so they'll have their own ice cubes and drinks in the back of the car and won't have to fight."

"Another solution."

"Right."

"And you'll have peace and quiet."

"We both will," he corrected.

She could tell he was trying not to laugh by the way his eyes sparkled. When had he become so cheerful? Jess gave up the argument and pushed the cart into the checkout line. "Are you like this all the time?"

"Like what?"

"Giving orders."

"Yes," he agreed, but his smile charmed her. "I'm also starting to feel normal again." He flapped his broken arm. "See? No pain."

"That's wonderful." The arm hadn't bothered him last night, either, from what she'd been able to tell. Jess felt better, too—no more drippy nose, no trace of sinus headache and only two days left to go on the antibiotic. "You're in shape for Fort Laramie."

"I'm susceptible to heat stroke, remember?"

"Tough." Jess unloaded her purchases onto the conveyor belt. "This is our big chance to see a fort."

"A fort?" Jeremy said, jumping with excitement. "We're gonna see a fort?"

Henry nodded. "Looks like there's a very hot one waiting for us in Nebraska."

"LOOK FOR A SIGN that says Scottsbluff."

Henry studied the map for a moment. "That's in Nebraska, right?" He didn't wait for an answer. "Route 26."

"Good," Jess said, glancing into the side mirror before passing the car in front of them. "We shouldn't be far away from that now."

"Probably about twenty miles to the turnoff, then another forty to that tourist place you want to see so much." He looked around to see what the children were doing. It was eerily quiet in the car. They were shaping worms and snakes from the clay and had them coiled all over the back seat, which looked like Whalens' Reptile World. The Whalen kids weren't fighting with each other and risking a spanking this morning, and Henry decided it was the best twelve dollars he'd spent in a long time. Maybe he'd gotten carried away by grabbing every box of clay on the shelf, but it sure beat scraping crayon wax off a duffel bag.

Henry turned back to Jess. She sang softly to a county and western song—what else was there? He couldn't hear the words: the wind rushing through the car windows drowned her out. But he watched her lips move, and she didn't falter over a single syllable. Amazing.

"You look ridiculous, you know." Affection softened the observation as Henry watched Jess reach into the cooler and grab a handful of ice cubes. She positioned the ice on top of the washcloth draped over her head like an old-fashioned mantilla.

"Thank you," she answered, unperturbed. "It's my own form of air-conditioning, and I have you to thank for the idea."

"I put the ice in the dishpans, not on your head." It was so hot the water from the melting ice evaporated before it could clear the washcloth and drip down her neck. She looked silly, but kind of cute.

"It feels good," Jess said with a sigh. "Almost better than swimming."

"And you stole the washcloth from the motel."

She carefully moved her head and smiled at Henry. "It has a tear. They were probably going to throw it away anyway."

Henry tossed the map on the seat beside him. "I can't believe this."

"Look" she said, pushing the sunglasses back on her nose. "If I overheat and get sick, then what are you going to do? Rent a Conestoga wagon and a couple of oxen?" There was a smug look on her face as she added, "Could you manage the reins with one hand?"

"You'd be surprised," Henry replied. "I have a way with oxen."

Jess laughed, and guided the car toward the Nebraska-Wyoming border. But there was no stockade when they finally arrived at Fort Laramie, only an L-shaped arrangement of low buildings. Jess followed the neatly painted signs and drove into the deserted parking area.

"We're in the middle of nowhere," Henry said.

"Think how the pioneers felt." Jess tossed the washcloth into the cooler and ran her fingers through her hair. Then she opened the doors and let the children pile out of the car. The white buildings looked like part of a movie set. The children chose to play outside while

Jess and Henry headed toward a building marked Visitor Information. Once inside, Jess wished she could remember the name of the movie in which John Wayne was in the cavalry. The gritty wooden floor reminded her of where John Wayne had danced with the colonel's daughter, who might have been Shirley Temple, but— "Welcome to Fort Laramie." An elderly lady handed Jess a pamphlet. "If you and your husband would like any more information about our fort, please ask."

"Okay." Jess looked longingly at a display of Western history books. "We'll be back."

"Come on, dear." Henry took her elbow. "Let's go show the children the barracks."

"All of the buildings are open for viewing," the woman called after them. "Please don't go past the roped-off areas."

"We won't," Jess assured her. The screen door bounced shut behind her.

Henry shaded his eyes against the sun as he looked around the grassy area. "Where's the jail? You seem partial to those, right?"

"Right."

He took her hand to lead her toward the nearest building. The kids ran across the grass to join them. "Come on," Henry said. "The sooner we do this the sooner we'll be back in the car."

Jess liked the feel of her hand tucked inside his. "I can't believe you don't have more respect for history."

Sue frowned up at her mother. "Why is he holding your hand?"

Jess opened her mouth, but no words came out. She wasn't sure why Henry was holding her hand.

"Because," Henry explained, "if I don't hang on to your mother, she'll go back to the information building and start buying books."

Sue sighed. "You better hold on real tight. I wanna see if they have any horses here."

"Go on," Henry said. "We'll catch up with you two in a few minutes."

"Still giving orders, I see," Jess murmured.

"Yeah." Henry gestured her to go through the open doorway of the officers' quarters and into the dusty barracks. "I need to stay in the shade, remember?"

"Stay in the shade by yourself then," Jess answered, trying to concentrate on the display of authentic military paraphernalia. "I want to be a tourist."

"Not now," Henry said, dropping her hand and encircling her nape. "Let's kiss for thirty or forty minutes until the kids find us."

Jess shook her head as Henry's lips drew closer. "Henry, about last night, don't you think—"

"Uh-uh." He brushed her lips with his own. "No thinking."

Another good idea. Jess closed her eyes, loving the warmth of his lips against hers. The tantalizing pressure against her mouth intensified, and she slid her hands behind his neck. His tongue teased her lips until they parted, allowing him to explore her mouth and tangle with her tongue for long, heated minutes.

Jess finally pulled away, but Henry kept her against him, dotting her neck with soft kisses until she thought she'd collapse onto the wooden floor. The passion he created was terrifying and wonderful at the same time, and Jess fought to regain some control over her feelings as she dropped her hands back to her sides and looked into his eyes.

"Why are we doing this?" she whispered.

His mouth turned down, and he tucked a stray strand of Jess's hair behind her ear. "I can give you a few reasons."

"Let's not do it anymore." She tried to put some conviction into her words, but was foiled by his fingertip trailing along her cheek and touching her lips as she spoke. "It's not a good idea."

"We could argue about that," he said, dropping his hand, "or we could look at moldy Army blankets and photographs of soldiers."

"I don't want to argue," Jess replied. She walked into the sunlit doorway and watched as the children, unaffected by the heat, chased each other around the flagpole. "I want to get back on the road."

HENRY DIDN'T HAVE anything to read. There was nothing to look at except the Nebraska plains, the sight of Chimney Rock in the distance had lost its thrill an hour ago, and the history book he'd purchased at Fort Laramie was more for Jess's enjoyment. He didn't feel like reading about this hot country when he was riding through it. Maybe, he thought, he'd brush up on his history when he was back in the cool, cloudy comfort of his Seattle town house.

He unfolded the map and studied Nebraska. Jess had been quiet since Fort Laramie, even during lunch. She'd been nervous about the restaurant he selected, but calmed down when she saw the prices weren't going to bankrupt her. The cool air, ice water and non-plastic eating utensils had been pretty easy to appreciate.

Henry wished she would talk to him. "It's not as hot today," he ventured.

"No, I don't think it is."

"Harrigan looked healthy this morning."

She nodded. "I think he's recovered."

"Sometimes I think I can smell the ocean."

She shot him an enquiring look. "You do?"

He shrugged. "I know it sounds crazy, but once in a while this car smells like low tide."

"It's the crabs," Jeremy piped up from the back seat. "They're under the seat."

Henry turned to look. "The *what* are *where*?"

"My hermit crabs," Jeremy said, winding a rope of clay around his finger. "They're in a bowl under your seat."

"Hermit crabs," Henry repeated.

"Hermie and Kermie."

"Don't worry," Jess said. "They can't get out, but they do get lively in the heat. I think they like it."

Henry turned back to the map, trying to forget there was a bowl of crabs under him. "Are we going to get as far as North Platte tonight?"

"Oshkosh," Jess said.

"Bless you."

"Very funny." But she smiled.

"Where is this place?"

"Look a few inches to the left of North Platte."

Henry awkwardly creased the map. "These are all small towns. Won't we have trouble finding a motel?"

"Uh, it's okay," Jess said. "That's all been taken care of."

"Why do I think there's something you're not telling me?"

"It's not a big deal, Henry. Don't worry about it." She rubbed her palms on the sticky steering wheel. Henry wasn't going to like this. It was going to be all downhill from now on.

"Then tell me." He gestured out the window at the arid landscape. "It's not as if we'll miss anything if we talk."

"You're getting grumpy again," Jess observed. "Why don't you climb into the back and make a clay alligator?"

"Don't try to change the subject. Personally I think

I'm a genius for coming up with the clay idea, but you don't have to say so if you don't want to."

Jess grinned at him. "You're a genius for coming up with the clay idea."

"Thank you. What a nice thing to say."

"Think nothing of it," Jess replied, sticking one hand in the cooler. She pulled a can of soda from the ice. "Would you please open this for me?"

He took it, popped the top and handed it back to her. "Where are we staying tonight, Jess?"

"At my sister-in-law's house." There. She'd said it. Now the sparks would fly.

"Why?" His voice was deceptively mild, and Jess didn't turn to look at him. She took a long swallow from the can, then pretended to concentrate on the open road ahead of her, as if it held four lanes of bumper-to-bumper traffic.

"I haven't seen her in years, and I wanted the kids to know they have some family."

"I'll stay in a motel. It's no problem."

"Yes, it is." Jess kept her eyes on the road. "We'll be in the middle of nowhere—they live on a farm—but it's a big farmhouse. I've seen pictures. I called last week and told them I'd have a friend with me." Silence. Jess watched two-tenths of a mile roll by the odometer.

"So, your relatives know I'm coming with you. Do they have room?"

"Sure. You'll like it."

"Right." He wanted privacy, the boxing matches on cable television and, especially, to kiss Jess good-night again. Kissing her good-morning would be even better.

"No, really, Henry," she insisted. "You will."

He lifted the lid of the cooler and grabbed a can of root beer. "Couldn't we just say hello, have a glass of iced tea and a couple of cookies, sit on the front porch, talk about the weather, then leave?" He knew the question was futile, but he waited for her to say something while he opened the can and drank.

"No. Don't you ever visit relatives?"

"I don't have any, except my brother and G.H."

"You're lucky to have G.H." Jess said. "He's so sweet."

"I wish you'd quit referring to him that way."

"Why?"

"He's the toughest old man I've ever met, and you make him sound like a doddering fool."

"That's not true," Jess protested, looking over at Henry. "I like him. Look how much he helped me by finding someone for us to travel with." As soon as the words were out of her mouth, Jess realized how stupid she sounded. The "someone" G.H. had found for her had been uncooperative, grouchy, bossy…kind, sexy and passionate. Too passionate. Had the old man done her a favor? Probably not.

Henry leaned back and tried to relax. They had miles to go before reaching Oshkosh, and he needed to think. G.H. was no fool. The old man had double-crossed him with the worst weapon of all—the truth. And he'd fallen into the trap nicely. Jess was no old man's honey, he'd bet his last nickel on that. Obviously, G.H. had known Henry would leap to protect his interests after the Las Vegas affair. Henry sighed, watching the scenery whip past. So what was G.H. up to? There had to be more to this than the old man being nice to his favorite waitress. It was time to call him and demand some answers.

"THIS IS GREAT!" A smiling young woman with short brown hair hugged Jess, while Henry and the children stood back and watched. "This is *so* great."

"Here, kids," Jess said, bringing them forward. "Meet your Aunt Amanda."

"You said to look for you this week, so I've been leaving notes on the kitchen door whenever I was down at the barn. I hope you didn't have any trouble finding us."

"No trouble at all," Henry said politely after Jess made the introductions. Jess had whipped a piece of lined paper from her bag and had driven down six bumpy dirt roads before discovering which way north was. Henry figured he was lucky none of his teeth had shaken loose.

"Come on, then," Amanda said. "We'll get Jeff out of the barn, give you a quick tour of the place and then have supper. It's all ready, just waiting for us."

Jeff turned out to be a tall, blond giant in faded overalls and a worn denim shirt. He looked like a good-natured scarecrow who had suddenly come to life. He accompanied them on their tour and then led them all back to the dining room table and a huge meal.

Hoisting a big spatterware bowl of mashed potatoes, Jeff handed it to Henry. "Have some more," he urged. "We're sure glad Jess brought a friend. This is quite a trip she's making."

"Yes, it is," Henry said, spooning another helping of potatoes onto his plate. He handed the bowl to Jess and she smiled at him, making Henry's stomach flip strangely. Must be the pot roast, he thought. "This is a delicious dinner," he told Amanda.

"Our own Nebraska beef," Jeff said with pride. "Best in the nation."

"I believe you," Henry said. "How long have you had this place?"

Jeff was busy helping the children scoop orange gelatin dessert onto their plates, so Amanda answered. "It belonged to Jeff's grandparents, and he was the only one in the family who wanted it after they died."

"It's always been home," Jeff added, handing Henry the platter of beef.

"Have as much as you want, Henry," Amanda said. "There's more where that came from." She looked at Jess. "At first I tried to fix up the inside of the house—there's a lot of painting and papering to be done—but I'd rather be outdoors helping with the livestock, so it's not real fancy."

"It's wonderful," Jess assured her. "Especially after all the motels we've stayed in."

"I'm so glad you can spend some time with us."

Some time? That sounded longer than just overnight. Henry tried to catch Jess's attention, but she avoided looking at him.

"You're excused," Jess told the kids. "Just be careful."

Jeff chuckled. "There's some chickens to chase and a whole mess of kittens in the barn. Those kids won't know what to do first."

Amanda wiped her eyes on her napkin. "Jeremy looks a little like Tom, Jess."

"C'mon, Henry." Jeff scraped his chair back and stood up. "Let's get out of this kitchen and I'll finish up outside. There's an hour of daylight left. Do you like boxing?"

Henry nodded. "Isn't there a fight on tonight?"

"Yep, and we don't want to miss it." He checked his watch.

"You have cable out here?"

Jeff chuckled. "No, sir. Look over there, out the west window." He pointed to a gleaming satellite dish. "My grandparents had that installed years ago. I couldn't believe they spent all that money, but there are lots of times, especially in the winter, when I'm glad they did It's a long drive to town to see a movie."

"Movies?" Amanda laughed. "More like Nebraska Cornhuskers football."

Jeff grinned. "Yeah. C'mon, Henry. They might make us help with the dishes if we don't get out of here. You can borrow a pair of my boots and water the garden."

"Bring back some more tomatoes, okay?"

"Sure, hon," Jeff called. "See you ladies in a while."

Later, when Jess was up to her elbows in soapy dishwater, Amanda grabbed a towel and stood beside her at the sink.

"Henry's a nice man," she said, grabbing a plate from the drainer.

"I'm glad you like him."

"I do." They worked in companionable silence for a few minutes. "It must be serious."

Jess laughed. "No. He broke his arm and needed a ride to New York."

"It must be serious," Amanda insisted, "for him to be traveling with you like this. When you wrote that you were trying to find someone to share expenses, I had no idea you were bringing a handsome man like that."

"Neither did I."

"How serious is it?"

"It's *not*. We're just acquaintances."

"He can't take his eyes off you."

Jess made a face "He's afraid I might leave him here."

"Well," Amanda said, sighing, "at least you haven't lost your sense of humor after all you've been through."

"I'm serious, Mandy. I hardly know Henry."

"You look like one big happy family."

"Looks are deceiving," Jess laughed. "You know, it's almost fun to wash dishes again."

"Don't change the subject. Tom would have been happy for you, Jess, if you decided to marry again."

"Maybe." Three years, Jess thought, was a long time to be alone. "But that's not exactly what I have in mind."

"I wish we could see each other more often." Amanda said. "It's so hard to get away from a farm, though."

"Any time you want to see ocean instead of prairie, come to New England." Jess rinsed the last pot and let the soapy water go down the drain.

"I put the kettle on for tea," Amanda said, pulling thick white mugs from the cupboard. "Or would you rather have coffee?"

"Tea's fine." Jess watched out the window as Henry watered a nearby garden. The kids sneaked up—trying to scare him, she supposed. But he turned around at the last second and sprayed them with water until they squealed and ran for cover in the barn.

Amanda put her hand on Jess's arm. "Stay for a few days, Jess. The entire second floor is yours—we never use it—so you won't be in anyone's way. Stay as long as you can and rest up. Take the weight of the world off your shoulders for a while."

"Thanks, Mandy. I'll think—" Jess stopped, watching Henry pick bright red tomatoes from the garden and put them inside his sling for safekeeping.

"Why, we'll make a farmer out of him yet, won't we?"

Jess turned away from the window. Another day or two on the farm would give her some distance from Henry. That was all she needed, Jess decided. A little space.

"WHERE AM I supposed to sleep?"

Jess tiptoed across the hall. "Shh! I just put the kids to bed."

He looked at the confusing maze of doors and hallways. "Where?"

"In bunk beds out on the screened porch. They think they're camping. Jeremy wants to hear the rooster crow in the morning."

"Amanda sent me up here," Henry whispered, "and said you'd show me where my room is." He gestured toward the wide four-poster bed in Jess's lighted room. "Does she think we're sleeping together?"

"She's trying to be discreet," Jess said. "I made up a bed for you across the hall. Come on." He followed her as she stepped into a dark room and switched on the overhead light. "There," Jess said, pointing to the double bed. "Now you should be all set. Good night."

He didn't stay in the room as she'd expected him to, but followed her back into hers. "How long are we staying here?"

Jess put her bag on the bed and unzipped it. "Just an extra day." She took out *Moving On* and placed it on the nightstand before facing Henry. "We've been traveling pretty hard. The rest might do us both good."

"Your family thinks we're a couple."

"I know." Jess sighed. "Just ignore it."

"Ignore you?" Henry stepped closer and put his hand on Jess's shoulder. He turned her gently to face him. "That's not so easy."

Jess resisted leaning into him. "Henry, please..."

"Please, what?" He tilted her chin with his index finger. "Please kiss me good-night, Henry?"

"You obviously think I'm more polite than I am," Jess said softly. "I've never said 'please kiss me good-night' to anyone."

"Please *don't* kiss me good-night?" His eyes danced with laughter as he leaned closer.

"I've never said that, either."

"What did you say?" he asked, brushing his lips against her cheek in soft butterfly kisses.

"My father told me to kick them where it hurts."

"Ouch," he murmured against her earlobe. "Should I risk it?"

"That's up to you." Her mouth curved in soft invitation.

"Well—" he slid his hand along her cheek and then tangled his fingers in her hair. "—you haven't hurt me yet."

She lifted her lips to meet his. He tasted sweet and hot, and Jess felt her own need mirror his. The kiss deepened into more than she had known she wanted, the passion quick and rising as he pulled her against him. His tongue danced with hers until she couldn't take any more and, afraid of the easy passion flaring between them, she pulled away. How could this man affect her so strongly? She stared up at him, the stranger she'd met only a few days ago. He nibbled a soft trail along her lower lip, caressing her cheek with his free hand before releasing her.

"You're not going to kick me, are you?"

Jess shook her head. "I don't know *what* to do with you."

His mouth turned up at the corners. "Don't feed me straight lines like that, Jess." He ran his hand through his tousled hair and rubbed his neck.

Jess longed to untie the sling and massage his shoulders. "I don't like what's happening between us."

He raised an eyebrow. "You don't?"

"All right," she said frowning. "I like it too much. That's the problem."

Henry only smiled at her. "'Night, Jess." He shut the

door behind him as he walked out, leaving Jess alone with her paperback book. She sat on the quilt that covered the bed. Its faded yellow starburst pattern was a puzzling maze of diamonds, and Jess traced the puckered stitches with her finger and wondered if she could hold herself together for a few more days.

7

JESS ESCAPED THE HEAT of the afternoon and slipped inside the empty barn. The sweet smell of fresh hay enveloped her as she walked past open stalls to climb the ladder to the haymow. The barn was old; coats of faded whitewash covered the worn boards, and various initials decorated the walls. Jess looked around with satisfaction. She needed a good place to cry, and this was the perfect spot.

She sat down at the edge of the loft and swung her bare legs over the side. Barn swallows sent shadows skimming over the roof, and sunshine peeked through slits in the walls. She heard the distant sound of the tractor and knew Jeff was back in the fields. Amanda had taken the children to town to deliver two kittens to their new owners, a job the kids had decided was more important than riding on the tractor with their uncle. Henry was taking a walk.

They would leave tomorrow. March ahead into the unknown, which didn't have a pleasant sound to it. Self-doubt crept in every time Jess stopped to think about what she was doing. She felt her chest tighten in unaccustomed panic as tears sprang to her eyes. Maybe, she tried to tell herself, just being in the middle of something big was the tough part.

"Jess? What's wrong?" Henry called from below.

She opened her eyes and glared down at the familiar man standing below her. Was there no privacy anywhere in the United States? "Nothing."

"You're lying."

"Go away." She pointed toward the barn door. "I'm having a good time being alone."

"Are we leaving tomorrow?"

Jess cleared her throat and attempted a cheerful tone. "Sure. It might not be first thing in the morning, but we should be in Iowa by tomorrow night, or at least pretty close to it."

He nodded. "Good."

"I'm glad you approve." Jess realized Henry wasn't wearing his sling. His chest looked wider in the white T-shirt, and the jeans he wore must have been borrowed from Jeff, because they were rolled up at the hems. There was something dangerously masculine in the way he stood looking up at her.

"Can I come up?" he said.

"No." It felt good to argue with Henry. Almost as good as crying, but not quite. She was safe, because a one-armed man couldn't risk the ladder. She scooted away from the edge and called, "Go away."

He ignored her. "I just wanted you to know that even though I didn't expect to have a good time here, I did anyway."

"Well, you watered the garden a lot."

"It seemed to be the only thing I could do. And I've eaten my weight in tomatoes."

"I noticed." She waited for a moment, then leaned over to peer down at him, but he'd disappeared. "Henry?"

"Over here," he said, coming from behind a mound of hay in the loft.

"How did you get up here?"

"There's a more civilized set of stairs in the back. The kids and I were up here this morning hunting kittens."

Jess sighed. "I thought I was safe," she muttered under her breath.

He was close enough to hear. "Not from me."

"Go somewhere else." Jess folded her legs in to her chest and put her head down. She felt foolish blinking back tears. But she wanted her husband back, she wanted her marriage again, and she didn't want to be alone anymore. She felt Henry's strong arm around her shoulders, and he held her against him.

His voice was low. "Panic setting in?"

"Homesick," she said in a tiny voice.

"For Idaho?"

"For my husband." Jess expected him to draw away from her then, but he continued to hold her tightly. She rested her head on his shoulder and tried not to cry.

"Talk to me, Jess," he whispered. "Tell me how you feel."

"Why?"

"Because...I care." He surprised himself by meaning that. He didn't have to confront his grandfather for the truth. He already knew Jess Whelan was no golddigging floozy out to con money out of old men. If anything, G.H. had used Jess in order to make his grandson forgo his workaholic tendencies and get some rest.

"Oh." She sniffed. "It's just that seeing Amanda again reminded me so much of Tom—my husband—and seeing Mandy and Jeff so happy and being with family again and... Oh, I don't know. I can't explain it."

"You don't have to," Henry said. He pulled her closer to him, marveling briefly at the fact that he was sitting in a barn in Nebraska trying to comfort a weeping woman. She didn't know how attracted to her he had become. More than attracted. He wondered if she would cry harder if she knew, or if she'd tell him to find his own way back to Seattle. At least she was letting him hold her. That was progress, he figured. They sat together in silence as her tears dampened his arm.

"Stop it," Jess said with a gulp.

"Stop what?"

"Rubbing my arm like that."

"Oh, sorry." He hadn't known he was doing it.

"Maybe you should just move over a little." Jess wanted to melt into Henry's arms and have everything be all right, but of course it couldn't be. She couldn't let herself think that way, even if he was acting so wonderfully understanding and kind. She was relieved when he moved over an inch.

"I don't have a handkerchief."

"That's okay. I came prepared." She dug a tissue from her pocket, sniffed and wiped her nose.

"Jess, about last night..."

"Don't, okay?" She didn't want to discuss kissing. She wanted to forget it.

"Why not?" He turned his head and his lips brushed her earlobe.

"Don't do that."

"Um," he said. "Nice ear."

"That tickles," she lied. His breath sent shivers along her spine.

He moved his lips along her jawline. "Nice face, too," he murmured. "Turn your head so I can kiss you."

"No." She looked up at him and frowned. "I kissed you last night and you got your hopes up."

His grin was wicked. "My hopes?"

"Don't be obnoxious. You know what I mean."

"Sure," he repeated cheerfully. "Hopes."

Jess sighed, looking into his wonderful green eyes. The truth was she wanted him terribly. She wanted him to fill up the empty space in her heart, as if love-making would cure everything, would make her uncertain future suddenly safe and secure. Making love with Henry wasn't the answer, and Jess knew it.

He bent to kiss her, a smile still on his lips when they touched hers. *Just a little taste,* Jess thought, *and only for a moment.* The moment went on and on as sensation took over and intense pleasure drove rational thought away.

When Henry fell backwards into the straw, pulling her on top of him, Jess went willingly.

"Is this hurting you?" she asked, her face only inches from his.

He grinned. "In ways you can barely imagine."

"I meant your arm."

"I know." Henry lifted the casted arm off the pile of straw and caressed Jess's back. "It's fine."

"Good." Jess propped an elbow on his chest and leaned her chin in her hand. The back rub felt heavenly.

"I feel sixteen years old again," he said.

"Was that the last time you were in a hayloft?"

He smiled lazily. "I think that was the last time I wore jeans that felt this tight."

Jess was suddenly conscious of her thigh resting on the hard placket of Henry's fly. "No comment."

"Wise woman."

"A compliment? I'm shocked."

"Mmm. Don't let it go to your head." He tugged on her hair to bring her closer, and Jess didn't resist as his lips sent warmth cascading through her body. Passion rose between them, hot and strong. His large hand swept through her hair and held her head down to his while his tongue plundered her mouth.

Searching fingers trailed along her neck and down her spine, heating the skin beneath her blouse. His hand dipped lower to sweep the roundness of her buttocks and Jess thought she'd melt from the exquisite torture of being touched. It had been so long. So damn long.

It was tempting to let it continue, even though she knew she should stop. She didn't want to use sex for comfort, just because she felt sad and lonely and missed her husband's body next to hers under the covers. She slid her hands past Henry's chest, intending to push herself away, but she grew weak when she touched the soft skin of his neck and instead laid a trail of kisses along his jawline.

"Henry," she murmured against his throat. "This is crazy."

His fingers stroked the bare skin of her thigh, slipped under the hem of her shorts and rimmed the lace edge of her panties. "No, it isn't," he argued in a hoarse voice.

She nuzzled his ear, inhaling a faint trace of minty after-shave.

"Your skin feels like silk," he said, sliding his fingers back and forth underneath the lace.

"Henry..."

"Shh," he said. "I can't concentrate when you talk."

She lifted her head to look into his eyes. "Concentrate? On what?"

"Seduction in a hayloft."

"At least you're honest about it." She kissed his chin. "We're not going to roll around in the hayloft anymore."

"Why not? Aren't you having fun?"

"That's not the point. We have nothing in common. You don't even like me."

"I've changed my mind."

"Why?"

"Your nose isn't red anymore." He proved it by kissing the tip.

"I like you, too, now that you're not so crabby."

"You cheer me up." Another wicked grin.

"Don't be crude."

"I'm being honest," he countered.

"Sorry, Henry." Jess really meant it. She loved the feel of his hands, loved the closeness of another body next to hers. "The last thing I need in my life right now is more stress. Getting involved with you and having...sex would be too complicated."

"It's already complicated, Jess, no matter what you say." His expression grew serious as he added, "With or without the sex."

"Not *that* complicated." Jess moved off him reluctantly, but she was determined to escape the devastating touch of his hands on her rear end. She didn't get far. Henry rolled onto his side, still holding her, so that they lay facing each other.

"Fun, isn't it?" he asked. He stroked her side, dipping along the contours of her waist and up to her shoulder to pull her closer.

Jess tried to ignore how neatly their bodies fit together. "I should have let you expire from heat stroke when I had the chance," she grumbled. But her lips parted for his kiss, and this time she kissed him back, tasting the sweet promise of his lips and wanting more than she could let herself take. She wriggled out of his arms. "I'm leaving," she said, scooting toward the ladder.

"Coward." He sighed. "What are you afraid of?"

"Making a big mistake," she answered. She gave him a long, level look before disappearing over the edge of the loft.

Henry sat up and attempted to brush the straw from his hair. He wished he could have locked Jess in the barn. Eventually she might have discovered he wasn't so bad after all. He stretched out his arm without pain. It felt great, though his groin ached. He knew Jess and her gorgeous thighs were going to drive him crazy for the next couple of thousand miles. She was beautiful, and smart, too, in a weird way. Although he couldn't imagine what on earth she was going to do in Connecticut.

Henry stood up and brushed off his jeans. It made him crazy to think Jess wasn't more concerned about her future. How could she be so calm about moving her family across the country where she knew no one, had no place to live and no job? And she was worried that *lovemaking* would complicate her life? Henry thought about that as he walked down the stairs and out into the sunshine. He recognized an excuse when he heard one. But he'd never rushed a woman in his life and he wasn't about to start now. He might be falling in love, or making the biggest mistake of his life, or both. So, if they both figured they were making a mistake, why be so hot and bothered about it? Close proximity, Henry decided, meant trouble.

He heard the tractor in the distance. Jeff was a lucky man—all he had to worry about was hay and rain and droughts and storms.

WELL, JESS THOUGHT, letting the kitchen door slam shut behind her. So much for peace and quiet and a good cry. *I am a coward,* she thought ruefully. She'd wanted to stay in the barn and go on kissing Henry till the cows came home. But Henry had wanted to make love to her right there, and that had scared her to death.

She wished she could figure out how to stay away from him. But given that he'd be taking up room on the car's front seat again tomorrow, avoiding him was impossible. Until New York that is. Until he started his new life—whatever that was—and she started hers.

I'm a coward, she concluded once more, opening the refrigerator and taking out a pitcher of lemonade. She was afraid to admit she was attracted to a man she'd only met a few days ago.

Attracted. What a wimpy word for passion.

"Passion," Jess said out loud, pouring herself a drink. "It's not going to kill you."

"I'm glad to hear that," Amanda said, coming in the door. "Who are you trying to convince?"

Jess laughed to cover her embarrassment. "Myself, I guess."

"Are you talking yourself into it or out of it?"

She shrugged. "I think I'm just trying to get used to it."

Amanda sighed. "Well, while you're getting used to whatever it is you're talking about, you might want to get the straw out of your hair. That's the first thing you need to do if you've been rolling around in the hayloft."

"It's that obvious, huh?"

She nodded. "Your hair and your pink face tell quite a story." Amanda set a basket of zucchini on the counter while Jess tried to comb the evidence out of her hair. "We delivered the kittens. The kids just ran off to see if Jeff would let them ride Mouse."

"Is Mouse a very tame horse?"

"She's so old she practically falls asleep just walking around."

"I think I'll go watch," Jess said.

"Henry's with them," her sister-in-law warned.

"Then I think I'll drink my lemonade and hide in here with you."

Amanda patted Jess's shoulder. "Pour me some, too, will you? This could be a long afternoon."

"THAT WAS FUN. They're nice people." Henry buckled his seat belt and turned to wave at Jeff and Amanda.

"Surprised you, huh?" Jess put on her her sunglasses and drove away, glancing in the rearview mirror at the farm they were leaving.

"Yeah, it did." He lowered the volume of the radio. "Must be hard to say goodbye."

She nodded. "They're the only family we have left." But she and Amanda had tearfully assured each other they would write and keep in touch by visiting more often. "They liked you, too."

"Did you remember Harrigan?"

"Sure," Jess said. "He's behind you on the floor."

"He liked the farm."

Was she hallucinating? What kind of a conversation was this? "How do you know, Henry?"

"He 'eeped' a lot."

It was so ridiculous that Jess's awkwardness disappeared. Maybe Henry, too, was trying to pretend nothing had happened in the barn. "I think we're about six hours from Omaha, and it's already three o'clock. We should probably stay here tonight, since we're getting a late start." She waited for an argument from him, something about driving until midnight and getting in more miles. But he opened the map without complaining.

"Fine" was all he said.

"I'd like to try to find a motel with a pool so the kids can swim and work off some energy."

"Fine."

She looked at him with concern. "Is your arm okay?"

"It's fine." Henry held out his arm and waved it back and forth. "No sling, remember?" He smiled, making Jess's heart flip-flop in response.

"Great," she managed.

"You could sound happier."

"Really, I'm happy for you," she said, but she was thinking that the loose arm made him more dangerous. He'd practically seduced her in the barn because he'd had the extra mobility. Jess fiddled with the radio dial until she found a clear station. An old Judy Collins song caught her attention.

"That's driving me crazy," Henry said after a long while.

Back to normal. How could he hate an easy-listening radio station? "What?"

"You know the words to every song on the radio."

"We talked about this before, Henry. I don't know what the big deal is. I was a waitress, the radio was always on, so I guess I learned a lot of songs."

"No kidding."

"What do *you* know a lot about?"

He stared at her. "What are you talking about?"

"What are you an expert at? Besides sailing, I mean." She took her gaze off the road and looked over at him. "What on earth do you—did you—do for a living?"

Henry didn't know what to say. "G.H. never told you?"

She shook her head. "I knew he had some kind of business in Seattle, but nothing more. He liked to talk about fish and gambling."

"Did he ever mention Muriel?"

"Who?"

"Never mind." Henry stalled, then realized it didn't matter whether she knew or not. "G.H. has a spice business."

"Spice? Like cinnamon, curry, nutmeg…?"

"Exactly. Importing, packaging and distributing."

"It must smell wonderful."

Henry thought of the new leather sofa in his office. "G.H. loves it, always has."

"Did you work for him?"

"No." Which wasn't exactly a lie. He'd worked with his father on development projects, such as marinas.

"Well, what are you going to do in New York? Look for work?"

"It's a possibility." Henry squirmed against the vinyl seat. How had he gotten into this mess of lies? He couldn't let Jess know he'd been lying to her all along, that he'd made up everything just to protect G.H. from her alleged fortune-hunting plans. He could only guess how she'd feel about that. She might kick him out, right here in the middle of Nebraska. And he'd just begun to have a good time. He stretched out his arm along the back of the seat, wishing he could touch her while he told her the truth. She might be so angry she'd dump him at the next Dairy Queen. "We need ice," he said.

"Okay. Let me know if you see a place to buy it. I'm just going to stay on this road until we can hook up to Interstate 80 again."

So, Henry didn't want to talk about his job. Maybe he'd had trouble working for his grandfather or maybe he grew tired of living in Seattle. Jess thought about it for a minute and gave up. If he wanted to talk about it, that was fine, otherwise she wouldn't pry. She didn't want to dwell on the restaurant business, either. She flipped the dial again, searching until she found what she wanted. "There," she said. "I'll bet you know the words to that one."

He listened. "The Beatles, right?"

Jess sighed. "No. The Rolling Stones." She turned up the volume.

"'Satisfaction,'" he pronounced, sounding pleased.

"Sing it to me, Henry." Jess laughed. "The chorus is pretty easy."

He did, in a respectable baritone. The children sang out the words with gusto, and Jess pounded the rhythm on the steering wheel. Harrigan chirped excitedly.

"Now," Jess said after the final notes had died down, "wasn't that fun?"

Later, at the gas station, Henry insisted on pumping the gas at the self-serve island while Jess dug the expense envelope out of the glove compartment. "We need to put money in this again."

"I'll take care of it," he called. Jess climbed out of the car and watched the children go into the bathrooms, then decided to wash the front windshield. A lot of bugs had died on the glass. She grabbed a squeegee from a bucket of water by the gas pumps and began scrubbing.

"I'll do that, Jess," Henry said, reaching for the squeegee. His hand closed around Jess's as he smiled down at her. "Why don't you just take it easy for a few minutes?"

She slipped her hand out from under his. Henry was standing very close, their bodies were almost touching, and he looked as if he was enjoying it. "All right," she said, backing up. Jeremy ran over, his face flushed with heat.

"Do you have any quarters for the soda machine?"

"In my wallet, maybe. Go look." She shaded her eyes and looked up at Henry. "We should stop in North Platte and get some more drinks and fruit."

"Is that a big town?"

"Looks like it on the map."

Jess escaped to the rest room on the side of the garage and splashed water on her face. She hoped that, after settling in New England, she would never have to use another grungy gas station bathroom for the rest of her life.

"I paid for the gas," Henry said, when she returned to the car.

"I'll write it down." She reached for the envelope.

Sue leaned over the seat. "Are we gonna swim tonight?"

"Yeah, Mom, just like in Missoula?"

Henry handed Jess a can of soda, then tucked his camera under the seat. "I told them we'd try to get a motel with a pool."

"Thanks," she said, touched by his thoughtfulness. She started the car and sped onto the highway.

"Can you swim now, Mom?"

"Sure." She looked in the rearview mirror at her son. "I'm feeling great." *As long as I don't think about making love to the man on the front seat next to me, I'm just fine.*

LONG HOURS PASSED, as Jess drove through mile after mile of Nebraska. She finished her second diet cola and placed the empty can on the floor. "Anybody hungry?"

"Me," Henry said. "Steak sandwich, large plate of fries and apple pie and ice cream for dessert."

Jess glanced at him. He was slouched in the seat looking as though he'd just woken up. "Are you serious?"

"Sure. It's dinnertime, isn't it?"

"You're sure cheerful today." She spoke out loud though she hadn't really meant to.

"Why shouldn't I be?" He tapped her shoulder so she'd look at him. "I'm feeling better, no more heat wave, no aching arm. Just you and me and the open road."

"Except it's not just you and me. There are two kids and a parakeet in the back. And two crabs."

"How could I forget?"

"Don't start complaining again," she warned.

"It was a joke, Jess. I think I might be having a good time."

"How can you tell?'

"Don't get cranky." He patted her shoulder. "Take the next exit—so we can get out of this car and find something to eat."

"Yeah!" The kids cheered in the back.

"They don't miss much, do they?"

Jess shook her head. "Not when it comes to food."

"I DON'T LIKE THIS," Jess muttered. "The air feels strange."

Henry peered at the darkening sky through the windshield. "Me, either."

"Don't agree with me. You're supposed to say something comforting."

"Sorry, but it looks like we're driving into one hell of a thunderstorm."

Jess gripped the steering wheel with sweating palms. "Where are we?"

"Just outside of Lincoln." He checked the map. "Another hour until Omaha, I think."

"I hate driving at night, and I especially hate thunder and lightning." Warm raindrops blew through the open window and hit her arm. "It's starting to sprinkle. You'd better roll up the windows."

"We're driving right into it, Jess. Hang in there—we don't have much farther to go." Gold threads of lightning streaked the sky close to the horizon and distant thunder boomed overhead. The kids screamed. "Lie down and put your earphones on," Henry told them. "Put the sleeping bag over your heads if you want. It will be over soon."

Jess wished she could put something over her head. It took all her self-control to keep her eyes open and see the boiling black sky ahead.

"You're doing great." Henry moved closer to her. His warm leg pressed alongside hers, a welcome distraction from the lightning.

She put the headlights on, noticing other cars doing the same thing. Torrents of rain blasted the windshield, and the wipers made a feeble attempt to keep the glass clear. She leaned forward, trying to peer through the sheets of water that coated the windshield. "I wish I could pull off the road."

"I'll help you look for a place, but it might be too dangerous. We could be rear-ended."

"Okay." The air inside the car grew stuffy now that the windows were closed.

"Just go slow, Jess." He rubbed her neck, massaging the stiff knots of tension above her shoulder blades. "Feel okay?"

"Uh, yeah." If it felt any better, she'd pull off the road and jump in his lap. A mile inched by.

"We should be out of this soon."

Jess knew he was lying. He didn't know any more than she did. "I hope so," she said. Could he hear the panic in her voice?

"You're doing fine."

Obviously he could. "Thanks." His hand soothed her; she enjoyed the feel of his fingers kneading her back and shoulders. When he rubbed her nape, Jess felt some of the strain ease. "We're going to make it through this, right?"

"Sure."

"I hate this sh—" Thunder crashed around them, drowning Jess's words.

Henry started to laugh until a bolt of lightning zapped into the ground beside the highway. Henry's hand froze on her neck. Jess felt the shock under her feet and gripped the steering wheel until her hands hurt. She felt as if she were waiting to die.

"That was close, wasn't it?" she whispered.

"Yes." His hands moved slowly along her neck. "Real close."

"That's what I thought." Her voice shook. "I don't know how much more of this I can take. I can hardly see."

"Do you want to pull off to the side now?"

"And just *sit* in this storm? No, thanks."

There was sympathy in his voice. "It can't last all evening, Jess."

"I don't care. I want to be indoors." *I want to pull the covers over my head and hide until morning.*

"We'll take the next exit." A couple of tense miles passed before Henry pointed out a green-and-white highway sign through the rain. "Let's try that," he said.

Jess guided the car onto the exit ramp and, after a stop sign, entered a small town.

"Over there."

Jess looked to the right. An older, one-story brick motel, its Vacancy sign lit, sat in a U-shape between a used-car lot and a row of stores. "Thank God," she sighed, and eased the car into the right lane.

"Is there a pool?" Sue yelled, popping up from under the sleeping bag.

Jess took a deep breath. "I don't think that matters right now, Sue." She stopped the car in front of the brightly lit office and Henry opened the door.

"Wait here," he yelled over the noise of the pounding rain, and dashed to the door.

Jess leaned back and listened to the rain. Thunder rumbled in the distance, but she didn't see any lightning. Maybe they should have kept going, driven out of the other end of the storm, but she was relieved to be off the interstate. *Please, let there be a room. Two rooms.*

Henry opened the door and leaned in. His hair was wet and water dripped down his face. "Good news," he said, panting.

"We're all set?"

"We have a suite," he announced. "We're lucky we stopped when we did. We got the last room, over there in the corner. I'll meet you."

We got the last room? He shut the door and Jess watched him jog around the walkway. It didn't take her long to park where Henry pointed. She told the kids to wait in the car, then ran through the storm to the open door of the unit. Henry turned on the lights to reveal a large room with double beds and a kitchen area. "How expensive is this, Henry?"

"We're sharing the cost, remember?" He peered into the other rooms. "It's not fancy, Jess."

"C'mon, Henry…"

"There's plenty of room for everyone, just like an apartment."

Jess stared at him. "I'm feeling a little awkward about this."

He came closer to her and put his hands on her shoulders. "We shared a room in Bozeman, remember?"

"That was different."

He shook his head. "Because we're very much attracted to each other?"

Jess decided not to answer. Spending the night in the same room with Henry after the episode in the barn didn't seem to be the smartest thing in the world to do. On a rainy night like this it was too tempting to think about cuddling up with someone to cling to whenever thunder crashed. Not just someone, Jess knew. Henry. She turned away from his touch. "I'll go tell the kids they can come in."

"I'm right behind you."

Jess stepped into the darkness and braced herself against the wind. Back to reality, she decided. It was time to concentrate on taking care of the kids and unloading the car. The tempting vision of being wrapped in Henry's arms on a stormy night would have to remain a fantasy.

8

"LOOK, MOM!" Sue called. "More bedrooms!"

"Just a second." Jess peeked into the black-and-white-tiled bathroom, where a tempting clawfoot tub filled half the room. Later, Jess promised herself, she'd sink up to her chin in hot water. She turned away and joined her daughter in front of a small room with a double bed and single nightstand.

"I told you it was nothing fancy," Henry called, setting the bird cage on the dresser in the main room.

Jess looked into the other bedroom as Sue ran off to join her brother in front of the television set. A larger bed filled the room; it also contained a television and an old green vinyl chair. "You have to tell me how much this place cost."

"Nothing out of our range."

"Baloney."

Henry grinned at her. "You really should trust me, Jess."

"Well," she said with a sigh, figuring she could pry the receipt from him later, "you pick which room you want."

He stood beside her and took her hand. "This one," he said, leading her into the larger private room with the television. "You're welcome to join me."

"I'll take the small bedroom, thank you."

He tugged her toward him, wrapping his arms around her. Jess couldn't resist leaning into him. His shirt was damp and smelled like rain. She closed her eyes and enjoyed being held.

"You feel good," he murmured, resting his chin on her head.

"So do you."

"Let's lock ourselves into this bedroom tonight after the kids are asleep."

"Sounds like an indecent proposition." But so tempting.

"Yeah." He chuckled. "Better than a barn."

Jess pulled away and looked up into his eyes. There was laughter there, but affection, too. "What I said in the barn is still true, Henry. No matter how I might feel about being with you doesn't change the fact that getting...involved with you right now doesn't make any sense." What didn't make any sense was why she was even spending time thinking about it at all, Jess thought silently.

"We're already involved, Jess. I don't know what's going on here either, except—"

"Mom," Jeremy wailed. "Do we get these beds?"

"Just a minute, Jer," Jess said, stepping out of Henry's embrace. "Guess I'd better go settle another argument about the sleeping arrangements."

Henry wanted to drop a quick kiss on her lips before she slipped away, but he stopped himself. "Are you hungry?"

"Hungry?"

"As in sending out for pizza."

Suddenly Jess was ravenous. "Sure. Do you think there's a place nearby?"

"There's an ad by the telephone. What do you want on it? I'll call." He touched her cheek. "Make love with me tonight, Jess."

"Pepperoni," she said. "I can't."

"One or two?"

"What?"

"Should I order one pizza or two?" He smiled, his eyes crinkling at the corners. "How about if we just sit in that ugly green chair and make out for an hour or two?"

"Mom!"

Jess edged toward the door. "Two."

"Hours?"

"Pizzas."

He sighed. "I should have known."

LATER, JESS WENT outside to get the map from the car. The rain still fell in torrents, so she didn't linger. She wanted to be back inside the room, where it was dry and comfortable. She wanted to be with Henry, who had made funny jokes all through dinner and yet studied her with a serious look in his eyes when he thought she didn't notice. He made her feel beautiful and desirable, and how many years ago had it been since she'd felt that way?

Jess sighed, opening the door to the suite. She'd better hide in the tub, read her book and hope Henry fell asleep early. She heard water running into the bathtub. Henry had claimed the tub first. Damn.

The children were tucked into their beds, so after Jess threw the pizza boxes in the garbage, she sat at the foot of Jeremy's bed to see what they were watching. It was another bloody adventure, with a group of soldiers trying to escape through the jungle.

"How can you watch this stuff?"

"It's neat, Mom," Jeremy whispered.

Jess turned to look at Sue. Her eyes were closed and her breathing was quiet. "Yeah, I can see how much your sister's enjoying it."

Jeremy grinned and pulled the blanket up to his

chin. "Do we have to get up real early in the morning? *Predator's* on next."

"That's no kind of movie for you. Doesn't everybody die in a swamp or someplace gruesome?"

"Everybody's seen it but me."

"You can rent it when you're older. Let's see what else is on beside this violent stuff." Jess leaned over and switched the channel. There had to be something the child could watch without being warped for the rest of his life.

"*Police Academy 5*!" he cheered, recognizing the movie. "I saw it at Danny's house one time."

"Aren't there a lot of four-letter words in that?"

"I don't listen to them," he said seriously. "I just like the funny stuff."

"Okay," Jess said, sighing. Comedy had to be better than murder. She lowered the volume, and turned off the lamp between the beds. The room was dark, except for the light coming from under the bathroom door, when she kissed her son and took her bag into the small bedroom to unpack. She pulled a clean oversize cotton nightshirt from the bag and shook out the wrinkles. Not exactly seductive lingerie.

Who am I kidding? Jess tossed the nightshirt onto the crimson bedspread. She wasn't going to fall into bed with Henry for a quick session of mad, passionate love-making. What on earth was she thinking? There were two children in the next room and she was a mother. *As if that makes a lot of difference,* said a voice inside. *Mothers don't have sex lives?*

This mother doesn't, Jess decided. Celibacy wasn't all bad. No diseases to catch, no fear of AIDS and no pregnancies. She sat down on the bed and stared at the wall. No love, joy or passion, either. No shared touches or the soft stroking of a man's hand and no delicious, heart-pounding, time-stopping orgasms.

Admit you miss that part of life. And while you're at it, admit you're scared to death you're falling in love. Jess shook her head, willing the voice to stop.

"Bathroom's free," Henry said, appearing in the doorway. "Why are you shaking your head?"

"Uh, just stretching my neck." Thank goodness he was dressed. At least half-dressed, with his gray slacks on. His beautifully muscled chest was matted with soft brown hair, his belt hung unbuckled and his feet were bare.

"I see you've picked your room," he said.

"Yep."

"Want to argue about it?"

"Nope." Jess stood and turned to grab her hairbrush and scoop the nightshirt from the bed. All she had to do was walk out of this room, take a bath, say a pleasant good-night to Henry and sleep in her chaste cotton nightshirt. Alone. Henry came up behind her and captured her around the waist with his casted arm. Jess lightly touched the plaster. "Doesn't that hurt?"

"No," he whispered into her neck. "I love holding you."

"We don't even know each other."

"That's a pretty feeble protest, Jess. You can do better than that."

She turned in his arms and faced him, the hairbrush forgotten in her hand. He smelled like soap. "I'm going to take a long bath and read my book now."

"Sounds boring."

"Sounds heavenly."

"Kiss me good-night."

"Now?"

He shook his head, his lips curving into a smile. "After."

"You must think I'm crazy. I'm not promising you anything."

His arms tightened around her. "Are you saying you can't resist me?"

"That's just wishful thinking on your part." She longed to brush her cheek against the soft hair on his chest, but she knew she'd be lost once she did. She kept her gaze on his face. He looked determined to get his own way. He was, no doubt, used to getting everything he wanted.

"Whatever you're thinking isn't very flattering to me, is it?"

"How did you know that?"

"Your eyes."

He could read her eyes now? Jess hoped nothing else showed. "I only thought you were used to getting everything you want."

Henry looked thoughtful. "That's not really true."

"And you want me."

He frowned. "What are you talking about, Jess? You make yourself sound like an object."

"I'm not up for a one-night stand."

"Who said one night?"

Jess shook her head. "I'm going to take a bath and you're going to bed."

"Jess," Henry said, holding her against him. "There's something between us, no matter how much you try to convince yourself there isn't. We've become more than acquaintances, and you know it." He ran his hand along the curve of her waist. "I touch you and something happens to both of us." He paused, his dark gaze on her face. "I get hard. You melt. I can feel you softening under my hand."

"Stop it, Henry." Her plea was a whisper. "Don't say any more." She pulled away from his embrace and fled the room.

JESS LEANED HER HEAD back against the porcelain and let the steaming water heat her skin. She didn't like the way this was adding up. Was she falling in love with Henry? The truth was right in front of her nose and she didn't want to see it. Because even if she did admit it, what difference did it make? And what was she supposed to do about it?

Getting out of the tub might be a start, she decided, pushing the lever to open the drain. She'd been in the bathroom for almost an hour, had read the same fifty pages of *Moving On* several times without being able to concentrate, and now hoped Henry was asleep. Fat chance. That would be too much to hope for. But Jess acknowledged, standing up and reaching for a towel, that she'd be disappointed if he was asleep. She liked being held and she liked being kissed and she'd probably like all the other stuff with Henry, too, but it was the grim thought of the morning after or the week after that bothered her.

Quietly she opened the bathroom door. She was wearing underpants beneath the yellow nightshirt; her hair lay in damp strands on her neck. Barefoot, she tiptoed through the large room where the children lay sleeping. Henry must have turned off the television when Jeremy fell asleep. His bedroom door was open, and Jess stopped when she saw him sitting on the floor in front of the television set. Propped by the foot of the bed, he had his legs stretched in front of him, and was drinking from a can of root beer.

"Come on in," he said.

Without the sling, Henry didn't look harmless anymore. He looked very masculine and appealing. Jess hesitated. "What are you watching?"

"An old John Wayne movie."

Jess stepped into the dark room and peered at the screen. John Wayne was trying to capture a rhinoceros.

"Want something to drink?" Henry rustled through

the cooler beside him on the floor. "I think there's another can of diet cola in here."

It was tempting. The hour in hot water had made her thirsty. "Sure."

"Have a seat." He patted the floor next to him.

Jess sat down, but not too close, and Henry handed her the can of soda. She told herself it was silly to feel so self-conscious, but she couldn't help it.

"What are you frowning about now?" he asked.

"Just thinking about the trip."

"It's hard to believe, isn't it?"

"What do you mean?"

"That the two of us are sitting here like old friends watching a movie together."

"Probably a big change from your glamorous nightlife in Seattle."

"You must have me mixed up with my grandfather."

"No dinners at the Space Needle? No moonlight cruises on the ferry?"

He shook his head. "Not really."

What did "not really" mean? she wondered, pretending to watch the movie. "I think I saw this when I was ten," she said.

"Come here." Henry put his arm around her shoulders. "This is the best part."

Jess scooted a fraction of an inch closer to Henry's hard thigh. Okay, so she liked the cuddling stuff. She was only human.

"We'd be more comfortable in bed."

"What a line."

"I'm serious," he said, but a chuckle made his chest bounce.

"Sure you are."

He gave her a very sincere look. "But we would be. We could prop the pillows against the headboard and sit on a nice soft mattress. The only thing we're missing is the buttered popcorn."

"Why didn't you sit on the bed to begin with, then?"

"I thought I'd scare you away, and you wouldn't watch the movie with me."

Jess wanted to laugh. "You were right. I wouldn't have."

He took his arm away from her shoulder and awkwardly climbed to his feet. "Come on, my darling." He laughed. "Let's go to bed."

"You want to rephrase that, Henry?"

"Not really. I'm hoping you'll get so comfortable you'll fall asleep and then I can have my way with you."

"Very funny." She stood up and helped him fix the pillows. "I'm not that tired." They sat together on the bed, the old mattress dipping and bringing Henry closer than Jess liked.

"Isn't this more comfortable?" He sounded pleased.

"Be honest, Henry. Was this really the last room available in the motel?"

"Cross my heart. You can look out the window and see if the Vacancy sign is still lit if you want."

Jess yawned. "I think I'm too comfortable to move."

He wrapped his good arm around her. "This is nice, isn't it?"

"Yes." She rested her head against his shoulder, and he began to plant soft kisses above her ear and along her hairline. "I think you should watch the movie," she said.

"You think too much," he murmured.

"That's not a very nice thing to say."

"Sorry." The feather-light kisses continued. "I should have offered to scrub your back tonight."

"I can scrub my own back, thank you." Goose bumps rose on her arms.

"It would've been more fun if I'd done it," he said. He trailed his fingers up her arm.

His touch was driving her crazy. Here she was, sitting on a bed somewhere in Nebraska, while a man she really cared about was trying to seduce her—and doing an excellent job of it. Jess didn't know how much more of this she could take. "Don't you want to see what John Wayne is doing?" she whispered. Whatever he was doing couldn't be as much fun as this.

"No. How about if I scrub your back after we make love tonight?"

"Who said we're going to make love?"

"Me. You." His lips touched hers, and Jess sank back into the pillows as his mouth brushed against hers in a slow, teasing motion. Finally, his tongue parted her lips to delve into the soft recesses of her mouth.

Jess curled her arms around Henry's neck, bringing him closer as the heated kiss continued. She wanted to go on kissing him, tasting the faint trace of root beer, inhaling the scent of his after-shave. When he lifted his mouth from hers, she realized she was lying on her side, her body only inches from his. She watched his lips tighten.

Worried she might be hurting him, she leaned back to look into his eyes. "Your arm..."

"I'm going to rest it right here," he said, laying the cast on the dip of her waist. "Too heavy?"

"No."

He bent down to kiss her again, once more taking control of her mouth. He didn't seem to be in a hurry, but Jess sensed barely controlled passion beneath the surface. He was giving her time, she realized. Time to sit up and say good-night. Time to explore the mounting passion between them. Time to say yes. She caressed his face with a gentle hand. Once, when he pulled his mouth away, she skimmed her thumbs along the moistness of his lower lip. Longing rushed through her, a longing to feel those lips on other parts of her body.

Henry pushed himself off the bed.

"Where are you going?" Jess could barely move. Her limbs felt like lead, but she twisted to watch him.

"To lock the door." His voice was hoarse. He stopped and turned around before reaching the door. "Unless you're leaving," he added.

Jess struggled to her knees. She slowly shook her head. "No."

He turned off the sound of the television, leaving the room bathed in dim light, then moved through the darkness to the bed.

With a deliberate motion, Henry slid his fingers over Jess's shirt. His thumbs circled her aching nipples, sending erotic messages along her skin.

"This has got to go," he murmured, slipping his hands under the hem of her shirt to lift it over her head. She helped him toss it aside, then his hands returned to stroke her breasts. "You're so beautiful."

Jess smiled up at him. "Stop it."

"Am I embarrassing you?"

"Yes."

"You are beautiful, you know. Don't smile—I'm serious." He tugged gently on one pebbled nipple. Longing stabbed through her, and she reached out to touch his bare chest. Her fingers tangled in the crinkly hair as his hands dropped to his waistband. He unzipped his pants and slid them off to stand naked before her.

"There's no doubt you're serious," Jess said.

He knelt with her on the bed. "I guess that's pretty obvious."

"Definitely." Her breath caught in her throat as he laid his naked body next to hers, and she felt the heat of him along her thigh.

Henry ran his lips along her cheek and found her mouth while his hands skimmed her breasts, touching the sensitive nipples briefly before sliding lower to find the elastic of her bikini underpants. His fingers dipped inside, playing with the fabric as he caressed her smooth belly. He was driving her crazy, and he knew it.

Jess reached for him, catching his hard length in her hand, smoothing the sleek skin with her palm. He groaned against her mouth. "Ah, Jess..."

He tugged the panties down and cupped her in his hand. Jess could feel herself swelling against his fingers as he stroked her tender folds.

No longer able to support herself upright she tumbled backwards, and they fell together onto the mattress. Kicking the bedspread to the floor they slid into crisp sheets. Henry trailed kisses along her skin, stopping at each breast to nibble and taste. He nipped at her waist with teasing lips, then moved lower to trail his tongue along her thighs before finding the damp vee between her legs that ached for his touch.

With lips and tongue he opened her, making her weak with desire, until she thought she would break apart from wanting him so much. Just as Jess thought she'd explode, he stopped, sliding up her body to lie alongside her.

"I have some protection," he said, and kissed her shoulder. "Do you mind?"

"No." She turned on her side to watch him as he rolled over the bed. "I'm not exactly prepared for this—it's been years." She could feel the blush heating her face. "I know that sounds ridiculous, but that's just the way I—"

"Jess, honey, you don't have to apologize." He returned to lie beside her. "You may have to do me a favor, though."

She felt the beginnings of panic—he was going to ask her to put a condom on him, and she'd never done it before. *You're a woman of the nineties,* she lectured herself. *You have to learn to do these things.* Trying to keep the embarrassment out of her voice, she asked, "What?"

"Come here," he said, pulling her toward him as he lay on his back. She noticed with relief that the condom was already in place. "I can't put my weight on my arm."

Understanding dawned and Jess straddled his waist. He guided her movements until, very slowly, he entered her. Her breath caught and she leaned forward as Henry rocked into her, his casted arm wrapped around her back. His lips captured her breast, and the rhythm took over, deep and thrilling, until Jess spiraled into release. In response, Henry's strokes deepened until he shattered inside her.

Jess collapsed on his chest, her body shaken by aftershocks. Henry nuzzled her neck as he murmured into her hair. His hand caressed her buttocks, gliding over the soft skin with smooth motions. Jess lifted her head and looked into the warmth of his eyes.

"Don't leave," he said.

"I'm too heavy for you."

He smoothed a strand of golden hair off her face and smiled. "I think you feel just right."

"So do you," she answered softly, conscious of the feel of him still wedged inside of her.

"That was fantastic," he said, gliding his fingers over her back. "But too short."

Jess wiggled. "Too short? I don't think so."

"Not that." He smiled. "The time."

She kissed his lips, tasting him with her tongue. "You have a stopwatch or something?"

"Mmm..." He sighed. "I want to make love to you for hours."

"I'm not going anywhere."

"Yes, you are." He lifted her off him and sat up, planting a quick kiss on her breast as she knelt by him.

"Where?"

Henry grinned. "There's a tub in the bathroom that's big enough for two people."

"Wrap the sheet around you," she cautioned as he slipped off the bed.

"Almost forgot," he said, grabbing his pants and tugging them on. Jess retrieved her T-shirt and pulled it over her head while Henry opened the door and peeked out.

"All clear," he whispered. They tiptoed across the dark room to the bathroom. The glow from the night-light outlined the tub. Henry turned on the water faucets while Jess locked the door. The sound echoed off the porcelain, filling the room with a roar.

"We'll have to be very quiet," Jess whispered.

Henry straightened, then turned toward Jess. He kept his voice low. "The first time I kissed you was in that bathroom in Montana."

"I remember."

"You practically ran out of the bathroom to get away."

"I couldn't believe it happened."

"Neither could I. I didn't know if you'd speak to me the next morning." He lifted the hem of Jess's shirt and pulled it over her head. Her perfect breasts were flushed pink. Henry grew hard just looking at her. The aching in his groin was becoming a familiar sensation around Jess. "You can get in first."

He watched as she settled herself into the steaming water.

"Too hot?"

She leaned back and closed her eyes. "Perfect."

He unfastened his slacks and let them drop to the floor before joining Jess. He rested his arm on the edge of the tub to keep the plaster safe from the rising water, then took the soap from the pocket in the wall. He traced a bubbly outline along Jess's shoulders, across her neck and lower, under the water to her breasts and belly. He lingered, caressing her as she relaxed against the end of the tub.

Henry loved touching her with such freedom. He tried to remember if he'd ever felt so free with another woman, but his brain refused to conjure up thoughts of anyone but Jess.

"You do a good job with one hand," she murmured, then opened her eyes and took the soap from him. "Now it's my turn."

Henry twisted to turn off the water, and the bathroom suddenly became quiet.

"I can't believe we both fit in here." She soaped his knees, scooting forward to let him stretch his legs. She skimmed the bar of soap along his furry thighs and higher. "Now we're getting to the good part," she said.

"I like the way you think," he said through gritted teeth as her fingers feathered his shaft for long minutes. Skin on skin. Henry throbbed against her palm. "Come closer."

Jess inched forward, her face beautiful in the shadowy light of the room as she gazed up at him. He kissed her, teasing her lips with his, as his body intimately brushed against hers. He forced himself to stop before penetrating her, contenting himself with swelling into her softness.

"You're teasing me," she whispered, still stroking him.

"It's the other way around."

"Oh, darn! I've lost the soap."

He groaned. "I hadn't noticed."

"Maybe we should scrub each other's backs instead."

"Not on your life." Henry planted a brief kiss on her shoulder before standing up. "Come on," he said, reaching to help her to her feet. "We're going back to bed."

Moments later, Jess snuggled next to Henry under the sheets. "Are we going to do this all night long?"

"I hope so," he answered, pulling her toward him.

"We both smell like soap."

"An aphrodisiac."

Jess sighed happily. "How am I going to drive all day tomorrow?"

"I'll sit close to you and rub your neck."

"Brilliant idea."

"I'm full of brilliant ideas," he whispered into her ear. "Want to hear another one?"

Jess smiled as she felt his hands on her once again. "Sure," she agreed, and reached for him in the darkness.

9

HENRY WOKE UP ALONE. He could hear whispered conversation outside the bedroom door, and realized he must be the last one awake. Light from behind the curtains filtered into the room, and he pulled the sheet to his waist when he saw the bedroom door open.

Jess tiptoed in, smiling when she saw that he was awake. She was dressed in shorts and a yellow tank top, ready for the day and looking as if she'd slept for twelve hours. "Good morning. I came to see if you were alive."

"I shouldn't be. Not after last night." Henry groped for his watch to see what time it was. Nine-thirty. He didn't know when he and Jess had finally drifted off to sleep, but it had to have been shortly before dawn.

She pretended to think that over as she handed him a cup of coffee. "This should help you."

Henry swung his legs over the edge of the bed and tucked the sheet over him before he took the coffee. "A real cup. How'd you manage that?"

"There's free coffee in the lobby, but they ran out of paper cups. I've promised to return this under penalty of death."

"You're a good woman."

"I think you said that last night."

"I meant it, in many ways." Henry set the cup on the nightstand and reached for her. As she stood between his knees, he pressed his face to her midriff, pulling up the top to nuzzle her warm skin.

"Henry..."

"You smell like soap again."

She laughed, running her fingers through his tangled hair. "You smell like sex."

"Is that good or bad?"

"Good," she groaned. "But you'll have to clean up. We should be on the road. Do you know what time it is?"

He shook his head, leaving a trail of kisses to her breasts. His lips traced the lacy edge of her bra, before he pulled her top down and looked up at her. "Obviously it's not time to make love to you again."

Jess almost weakened when she saw his arousal reshape the sheet. "Obviously it is, but we can't."

"Lock the door?"

She stepped back before she could be tempted to fall into his lap. "Uh-uh. The natives are getting restless. They're fighting over the doughnuts I bought next door. If you hurry there might be a few left."

Henry knew when he was defeated. "How soon do you want to leave?"

"Twenty minutes?"

He winced, and reached for his coffee. "I'll be ready."

Within thirty minutes, the last of the bags were loaded in the car, and the bird sat safely in his cage behind the front seat. The children rolled down the windows to gaze longingly at the swimming pool, while Henry climbed into the car.

"Great timing," Jess said. "I think the kids were about to mutiny."

"I'll join them," he said, looking back at the motel as Jess drove out of the narrow parking area. "I'll always remember this place."

Jess brought the car to a stop before venturing out

into the street. She looked over at Henry, and their eyes met. "Me, too."

He reached for her hand and squeezed it gently. "On the road again." He sighed. "We could make it a short traveling day."

"Yes, we could." Jess turned the car onto the ramp to the interstate highway. Acres of green fields stretched out on either side of the nearly empty road.

"The kids could swim and wear themselves out."

Jess shot Henry an impish grin. "True."

"We'd all have to go to bed early."

Jess laughed. "You're just full of good ideas this morning, aren't you?"

Henry nodded and leaned over to turn the radio on. "I might even feel like singing."

"Oh, good. Find a country station."

"I'll never be that cheerful."

WHAT WAS LEFT of the morning passed quickly. They stopped at a McDonald's for breakfast, then bought more ice and cold drinks for the coolers. Soon, just outside of Omaha, Jess spotted the Welcome to Iowa sign.

"New state!" she called.

"What?" Sue said, popping up from behind the seat.

"Iowa," Jess replied.

"How big is it?"

"Here," Henry offered. "I'll show you on the map."

Susan leaned over the seat to see. He pointed out Iowa.

After studying the colorful map for a long moment, Sue observed, "We're halfway there, huh?"

"Yes, I guess we are," Henry answered.

Jess realized the child was right. And halfway there didn't sound very good. Here she was in danger of falling in love with a man who was only good for another 1400 miles, like retread tires. Maybe, Jess fretted, 1400 miles was optimistic; it might even be less than that. She'd have to look it up on the map tonight, if she had a chance.

She sighed, concentrating on negotiating the thinning traffic. Forget the map. She'd rather spend time tonight making love with Henry than figuring out how many miles were left until she never saw him again.

Henry's voice cut through her worried thoughts. "You have job interviews set up in Connecticut or Rhode Island or wherever, don't you?"

"Sort of."

"Sort of?"

"Several agencies said they'd be happy to talk to me. All I have to do is call once I know when I'm going to be in the area."

"It takes a long time to get started in sales, you know."

"I know." Did he think she was stupid? "I told you before I have it all worked out."

He twisted on the seat to face her. "But are you sure you know what you're getting into?"

Jess was glad her sunglasses hid her eyes. Then again, she thought, maybe he should see how much he annoyed her. She tipped the glasses down and looked at him. "Excuse me?"

"For what?"

"Don't be dense," she said. "You're acting condescending again."

She stared ahead at the road while he sat silently beside her. Iowa spread out in front of her, but there wasn't much to see at the moment. She heard Henry clear his throat.

"I'm just curious about your plans," he said patiently.

"We've talked about this before. Why bring it up again?" Jess's stomach reknotted itself. *One thing at a time, Whalen. Get through the trip before you panic over part two.*

"Now who's being dense?"

"What do you mean?"

He glared at her. "I might possibly care about what happens to you."

Jess stared at him for as long as she dared. "Henry, don't. Don't make this into more than it is."

She looked back at the road in front of her. After a long moment, she heard Henry's low voice. "You're right," he said.

Jess's heart sank. She would have liked him to argue about it.

"MY EAR HURTS," Jeremy moaned, hanging over the front seat.

"Really hurts?" Jess asked. Jeremy had spent the past winter fighting one ear infection after another. "Henry, feel his forehead and tell me if he's hot."

Henry looked up from the newspaper. "How?"

"Just put your hand on his forehead."

Henry tried. "I think so. His face is hot."

"Uh-oh." Jess sighed. "Poor Jeremy. Here we go again. Honey, have something to drink and I'll get you something for the fever in a few minutes."

"Okay. I hope Sue didn't drink all the orange soda.'

"Henry, where are we?"

He looked up from the newspaper again. "Somewhere between Des Moines and Davenport."

"Could you be more specific?"

"Why?"

Jess tried to be patient. "I need to get Jeremy to a hospital and get his ears checked. He's going to need an antibiotic."

Henry unfolded the map and then studied the exit signs. "We're an hour away from Davenport, which is close to the Illinois border." He checked his watch. "It's already after four o'clock."

"Let's stop at Davenport, then. With luck there should be a hospital or clinic we can go to."

TWO HOURS LATER, Jess and Jeremy trudged across the hot hospital parking lot. Jess tucked the bottle of antibiotics into her tote bag and slipped on her sunglasses. She could see Henry leaning against the station wagon on the far side of the lot. When they reached the car, Jeremy climbed in the back seat and lay down.

Henry draped an arm over Jess's shoulder. "How are you doing? Want to call it a day?"

"Sure," she said, relaxing into his embrace. "If we can find a place to stay."

"I already did."

"No wonder I like you so much. How'd you do it?"

Henry guided her to the opened car door. "No genius involved, Jess. I can still punch the buttons on a pay phone. While you were in the emergency room, Sue and I had ice cream and made reservations." He tucked her behind the steering wheel and smiled down at her. "Wait till you see the pool."

JESS OPENED THE DOOR connecting the spacious rooms. Her bare feet sank into the beige carpeting as she stepped into Henry's room. "How much did this cost?"

"Don't worry, Jess," Henry said, pulling neat piles of clothing from his bag and placing them on the king-size bed. "It's all taken care of."

Jess glanced out the sliding glass doors toward the sparkling pool. The entire place was gorgeous, right down to the makeup lights over the bathroom mirror, which might mean disaster to her budget. "We're splitting the bill," she reminded him.

Henry looked at her and sighed. "Come on, Jess Forget it."

"No." She put her hands on her hips. "How much?"

Henry told her, decreasing the price by thirty dollars.

Her eyes narrowed. "No way. Show me the receipt."

"I'll find it later." He turned back to his unpacking.

"Henry..."

"Look," he said, hoping to put an end to the discussion. "We've been compromising. I ate breakfast at McDonald's this morning, didn't I?"

Jess nodded, trying not to smile. "You didn't gripe for more than five minutes."

"See?" Henry walked over to her and wrapped his arms around her waist.

"I guess that was an improvement."

"Of course it was," he assured her, tickling her earlobe with his lips. "Let's take the kids to the pool, send out for dinner, then—"

Jess wriggled closer, sliding her hands up his back. "Then?"

"Then I'm all yours." He nuzzled her neck. "We'll go to bed early." His arms tightened around her and he lifted his head to stare into her warm brown eyes.

"Henry, the kids are in the next room and the door's open," she warned. "What if they walk in?"

"I don't think they'll mind. Besides, they don't seem too concerned about anything but food, clay and swimming pools."

She wondered if that could be true. "They've been through a lot, leaving their home and their friends."

"They seem pretty well adjusted to me." He kissed her briefly. "They're just normal kids, worrying about what movie is on television, and whether or not you'll let them see it."

"I thought you didn't know much about children."

"I don't." He massaged her back, wishing he could feel her bare skin. "But I'm learning."

Jess tugged herself away from his embrace, sending him an apologetic smile. "Gotta go."

He walked with her to the doorway. Entranced by the flickering television screen, the children were seated on the edge of one of the large beds. They held white towels and had their swimsuits on. Jess shot Henry a you-may-be-right look. "Meet you at the pool?"

"Sure. I can't wait to ogle you while you swim in that sexy black bathing suit," he whispered.

"It's just a plain old suit," Jess protested.

He shook his head. "I remember the way you looked in Missoula, lying by the pool with the tissue box beside you."

"That seems like months ago." She wished she could lean into his chest and close her eyes. "See you in a few minutes."

"Right." His fingertips traced a regretful message along her spine before he turned back to his room.

She walked over to the bed. "Jer, honey, you know you can't go in the water—you have an ear infection."

"Mom! That's not fair!" He turned stricken eyes on her. "I feel fine."

"Twenty minutes ago you were asleep in the car. And you might still have a fever." She sat on the bed beside her son and touched his pale face, thankful that he wasn't as hot as he had been earlier.

"No, I don't."

"No, you don't, but you still can't go in the water." She stroked his hair. "You can sit on the edge of the pool with Henry, if you want."

Jeremy's eyes filled with tears. "It's not fair. We get a pool and I can't go in!"

"How about if I tuck you into this bed, and you can

watch anything you want? I bought some more orange soda, and you can drink it all, if you think that would taste good."

Sue tried to help. "I got your stuff out of the car for you. Want your G.I. Joe guys?"

Jess watched her son struggle with his disappointment. "Okay." He sighed. "Tell Henry he can watch *Die Hard* with me again if he wants."

"I will," Jess promised. "Let's get you under the covers."

Jeremy jumped off the bed and picked up the bird cage. "Harrigan can watch, too," he said, resting the cage on the bedside table. Harrigan happily flipped upside down on his perch. "He likes TV."

"Great." Jess turned down the covers and helped Jeremy fix the pillows. "I'll get your medicine."

"Did someone say *Die Hard*?" Henry stepped through the doorway. A white T-shirt hung past his waist; deep blue bathing trunks topped his muscular legs.

The child's face lit up. "Yeah, Henry! Wanna watch? It just started."

Henry didn't even hesitate. "Sure. We'll let the women hang out at the pool by themselves." He bent over and dragged the cooler next to the bed, then popped the lid off. "Orange or root beer?"

"Orange."

"Here, Jer. Take this first." Jess handed him a tiny plastic cup with pink liquid inside.

He drank, then made a face. "Yuck."

"Here," Henry said, handing him the soda. "Kill the taste."

Jess touched Henry's arm and gave him a grateful look. The small kindness he'd shown Jeremy touched her heart. "Have fun, you guys," she told them.

Sue bounced near the door. "Come on, Mom. Get your suit on."

Jess rummaged through her bag until she found her bathing suit. It would be a good idea, she told herself while changing her clothes in the bathroom, to put some space between Henry and herself. She could become too accustomed to having him around.

JESS SAT AT THE DESK studying the road atlas; she'd given up attempting to count the miles left to travel. The states seemed to be getting smaller. Was that good or bad? She'd have to give it some thought. Anyway, Jess knew she was running out of miles, running out of time.

She heard the sound of the shower coming from Henry's room and wished she could join him, but the children were still awake. Jess didn't share her body lightly; Henry was the first man since her husband died. With two children to raise and a household to support, Jess's priorities hadn't included a sex life.

But now here she was on the open road, with more freedom then she'd ever had in her life. The money was stretching nicely, job interviews waited. Even if the real estate business didn't work out right away, tourist areas like the New England coastline could use another experienced waitress. As long as she didn't have to waitress for the rest of her life, working crazy hours with aching legs, Jess figured she'd be okay. At least she would have a choice. That was what this trip was all about. There hadn't been any choices left in Idaho.

She closed the atlas and looked at the kids. They were giggling over the same Chevy Chase movie they'd watched a few days ago. Jeremy lay burrowed in a mountain of pillows, and Sue, cheeks pink from the sun, was snuggled in her own bed. They didn't act too upset about moving east. Having Henry around had helped. Once he'd cheered up. Once he'd relaxed. Once he'd come up with good ideas and gotten into the swing of traveling. Once he'd kissed her…

Lord, that man could kiss. Not in that love-'em-and-leave-'em way, either. Straight from the heart. The man ran deep, Jess knew. There would be no way to know what he was thinking unless he decided to tell her.

She pushed back the chair and climbed onto the bed beside her daughter. She took a pillow and propped it against the headboard, hoping her presence would lull the children to sleep.

Sue patted her hand. "Night, Mom."

"Night, hon," Jess murmured. She stretched out on the soft mattress and sank into the pillow. In minutes her eyelids grew heavy.

SOFT PRESSURE on her lips woke her. "What—"

"Shhh," Henry warned. "You'll wake the kids."

He sounded like a husband, Jess thought, struggling to wake up. Foolish thought. She opened her eyes and stared into his. "Henry?"

"Who else?"

Jess moved her stiff neck. The lights were off and the room was quiet. "I guess I fell asleep."

"Come do that in my bed," he whispered, brushing his lips against hers once more.

"I don't know," she said with a sigh, immediately warming to his touch. Common sense warred with passion. Why shouldn't she enjoy being with this man? Jess struggled to sit up, and swung her legs over the side of the bed. "What time is it?"

"After ten," Henry answered, offering his hand. He was bare-chested, naked except for a pair of blue running shorts.

Jess turned away from the tempting sight of his muscled chest and tucked the covers around her sleeping daughter, then stepped around to the other bed to feel Jeremy's forehead. To her relief, his skin was cool, his breathing soft and regular.

"How is he?" Henry asked, waiting by the door.

"Just fine." She followed Henry into his room. A lamp glowed in the corner, and the covers on the huge bed had been neatly turned back.

"I'm locking the door," Henry said.

"What if I can't hear the children?"

"We'll open it later," he assured her.

Jess was too sleepy to argue as Henry wrapped her in his arms. It felt so good to be held. She closed her eyes and inhaled the soapy scent of his skin.

Henry's voice rumbled near her ear. "All day I've thought about making love to you."

Jess chuckled, deciding she might as well admit it. "Me, too. It was a long day, wasn't it?"

"Too long," he agreed, trailing kisses along her ear. "I love your hair."

"My hair?"

"Yes," he murmured, trailing his fingers through the soft strands. "It's what I first noticed about you."

Jess tilted her head back to look into his face. "Not my red nose and watery eyes?"

He smiled. "Those, too."

"You must have thought I was crazy."

"I still have my doubts."

"Don't start—"

"You *are* crazy to move somewhere you've never even seen before."

Jess touched a finger to his lips. "Let's not get into this now. We can talk about it later, when you're too tired to argue with me."

"All right." He chuckled, squeezing her shoulder. "I'm ready to be exhausted."

She resisted when he tried to tug her toward the bed. Instead, slowly and deliberately, she slipped her hands inside the elastic waistband of his shorts. She tugged the fabric downward until the shorts fell to his ankles. He kicked them aside and for long moments Jess caressed the smooth, sensitive flesh that was now exposed to her touch.

Henry groaned. "Sit on the edge of the bed," he rasped, easing the nightshirt off Jess's body. "This damn cast..."

After Jess sat down, Henry knelt before her and gently parted her knees, planting kisses along the soft golden curls.

His lips and tongue wove ribbons of desire through her. She leaned weakly back on her arms, aching to have him inside of her as he continued his electrifying assault. But then passion burst inside of her and she arched helplessly against his mouth.

Long seconds passed, and Jess felt him move away. When she opened her eyes, he had joined her on the bed. She curled up next to him, loving the feel of his body alongside hers.

"My turn," she whispered, leaning over to smooth her hands along his chest, her lips following the trail, until she reached the hollow beneath his hips. He swelled against her cheek and she took him into her mouth with agonizing slowness, running her lips over the sensitive dome and capturing him inside of her mouth. She continued the loving motions until he groaned and lifted her away. They lay on their sides and smiled into each other's eyes.

"I can't believe how good we are," Henry said, as he fit himself into Jess.

"Neither can I," she gasped as he rocked inside her. His strokes grew harder, piercing her with intense pleasure, until she shattered around him. His lips muffled her cries as he held her closer and then found his own release.

Later, when he could speak, he said, "It's never been like this before, Jess. I just want you to know that."

"I know." Jess traced his smooth jaw with a delicate finger. *It's because I love you,* she wanted to whisper. *And because you might just be falling in love with me, too.*

DURING THE EARLY-MORNING hours, Jess slipped out of Henry's bed and put on her nightshirt. Snoring softly, Henry was lying tangled in the sheets. The sight of him made Jess marvel at how wonderful it was to sleep with a man again, to have another head on the pillow beside hers, to have the comfort of another human being when fears surfaced in the night.

She stood in the darkness, reluctant to open the connecting door and leave Henry's warmth. But she would have no answers for the children when they asked why she slept with Henry now. It wouldn't be right to force them to understand.

Later, after she'd checked to make sure Jeremy's skin was cool, she gently nudged Sue to her half of the bed and slipped under the covers.

10

"I WONDER if I could drive one-handed."

Jess looked over the seat to see Henry assessing the steering wheel, a thoughtful expression on his face.

"Don't even think it," she warned, fixing the cover on Harrigan's cage before shutting the car door.

He wriggled his fingers. "You must be tired of driving."

Jess slid behind the wheel and started the car. "It's already after ten. We'll make it a short day."

"Can we get a pool again?" Sue called. "That was really fun."

"Don't tell me about it," Jeremy moaned. "I don't wanna hear it."

Jess looked in the rearview mirror. "You'll be better soon, hon. And there'll be an ocean to swim in when we get to our new home."

"You look for the golden arches," Henry suggested, opening the map. "I'm going to figure out where we should stay tonight."

"We're not even out of the parking lot yet," Jess said. "You're really thinking ahead."

Henry slipped his hand along her thigh. "Hurry up and drive."

"I don't even know what day it is," Jess said. "That's scary." It was also scary to feel what his hand was doing to her. She tried to concentrate on finding a place to eat breakfast.

"It's Saturday. We've been on the road a week."

"Feels like longer, somehow." Jess pushed his hand away. "Stop it, Henry, or I'm going to rear-end that bus in front of us."

Henry moved away, turning his attention back to the map. "Let's try to make it to South Bend."

"What state?"

"Indiana. Looks like that's only about 250 miles away."

Two hundred and fifty miles was practically next door. She couldn't resist teasing Henry as she turned into the McDonald's parking lot. "Fine with me, but aren't you in a hurry?"

He ignored her question. "Tomorrow we're going to find one of those places that serves a Sunday brunch buffet. All you can eat. On china plates."

"In South Bend, Indiana?"

He nodded. "And we're going to sleep late, too."

WHEN HENRY WOKE UP on Monday morning, he knew they'd be crossing the Pennsylvania border shortly after getting on the road. Pennsylvania happened to be a wide state, thank goodness. But not nearly wide enough, at least not enough miles for a man to make up his mind about his future. He'd sat in the darkness long after Jess drifted off to sleep, trying to find some answers. Then it had hit him—all he needed was a phone book and a prayer that Alan's number was listed.

Jess's consent wouldn't be easily won, either. She was too damn stubborn. Every time he thought of her alone in a strange town, his heart constricted. He knew she was strong and capable, but he felt compelled to question her logic. Was moving to New England what she really wanted to do with her life? If she'd asked him, would he have said the hazy future benefits might not be worth the fears and probable struggle. But she hadn't asked him. Every time he tried to discuss the subject with Jess, she gave him a dirty look and insisted he mind his own business.

So now it was morning and he was the only one awake. By the time he had walked to the restaurant next door for a thermos of coffee and a box of doughnuts, it was almost eight o'clock. He quietly unlocked the door and opened the drapes.

Jess lay sleeping with Sue. He knew she'd never stay all night with him, because it wouldn't be right to do that in front of the children. He didn't know what kids understood about such things, but he could guess they'd be mixed up. And why not? How often did Mommy share a bed with a man? Never, Henry knew. Not unless you called him Daddy and made him a card on Father's Day. *Daddy?*

His own father wouldn't understand if he could see his son now. George had worked himself into a fatal heart attack, because he was too busy to go to the hospital to discover what was causing the pain in his chest. G.H. would be the one to laugh. "Enjoy yourself, son," his grandfather would cackle. "Live a little."

His father would have said, "Who's taking care of business?"

The truth was, Henry decided, pouring himself a cup of coffee, he hadn't thought much about business at all recently. He'd called Martha at the office last night, while Jess was swimming. Business was going along as usual. The young assistant he trained last winter had proved capable enough to handle the daily crises, and Martha controlled everything else. Henry realized he'd fallen into the role he'd made up for Jess—between jobs, he told her. The deception would have been funny if he hadn't loved her so much.

Loved her? Henry watched Jess sleeping, her hair spread over the pillow, a light pink blush on her cheeks. She was kind and funny and smart and beautiful...and she put up with him. She hadn't given in when he acted crabby, she'd helped him when she saw he was in pain, and had made love to him when he wasn't. And, Henry thought with a sigh, she fought him whenever he tried to discuss her future. What the hell was he going to do?

"WHAT DO YOU THINK?" Henry asked, after he'd explained his plans.

"Well," Jess drawled, reluctance in her voice, "I guess that would be okay."

"I stayed at the farm," Henry pointed out.

"True."

"You could give me one night with an old college buddy."

"I already agreed, Henry. You don't have to talk me into it any further." The grip of tension around Jess's heart eased. Secretly relieved, she kept her face expressionless. An extra day felt like a reprieve.

"Great."

"Is there a town near here? The kids and I will stay in a motel and pick you up tomorrow."

"No problem," Henry said. "Alan invited us all to stay at his house."

Jess shook her head. "No way. His wife must be having a nervous breakdown trying to figure out where to put company on such short notice. I can't do that to her."

"Nonsense." Henry studied the paper he'd written directions on. "Take a right at the next stop sign and go up a hill."

"Have you been here before?"

"Not the new place."

Minutes later, Jess parked in front of the oldest house she'd ever seen. The "new" place turned out to a pre-Revolutionary mansion. Jess could only stare at the brick facade and the tiny paned windows.

"Some house, huh?" Henry asked. "I saw a picture of it on their Christmas card last year."

"It looks like one of those George Washington Slept Here houses."

"George probably owned the place."

"Wow," Sue breathed in awe.

Jeremy hung over the front seat. "George Washington was a President, huh?"

"Yes, Jer. I don't know if he owned this house, but he spent a lot of time in this area during the Revolutionary War."

Jess sat frozen. "I don't know about this, Henry."

He grinned at her. "Don't worry. Al said there was plenty of room."

"He did, huh? But what if the kids break something? That's the kind of house I've seen in magazines. It's probably filled with antiques."

Henry shook his head, and opened the car door. "Trust me, it's going to be okay."

"Famous last words," Jess muttered, still unconvinced.

The mansion's door swung open and a short, slender man hurried down the steps. "Henry!" He hurried across the immaculate green lawn.

Henry climbed out of the station wagon. "Al!"

"You made it to Pennsylvania. I can't believe my eyes!"

Henry's friend was a slightly built man, with short chestnut hair and thick glasses. Jess slowly got out of the car while the two men embraced. Jeremy and Sue rushed to escape the confines of the car.

"It's been years," Henry said.

"Too long." Alan smiled at Jess. "Introduce me to your friends."

Henry put his arm on Jess's shoulders. "Jess, meet an old friend, Alan McCabe. Alan, my chauffeur, Jessica Whalen, and her children, Jeremy and Sue."

The children said hello, and Jess shook Alan's hand. "It's nice to meet you. I hope this isn't an imposition."

"Not at all, Jessica. I'm very happy to meet all of you, and Lily's had the housekeeper get everything ready for you." Alan slapped Henry on the back. "How'd you hurt your arm? Is that why this lovely lady is stuck driving you around the country?"

"It's a long story," Henry answered. He walked with Jess toward the house.

"How? Sailing?"

"Yeah. I'm hoping one of your colleagues will take the cast off."

Alan frowned. "How long has it been on?"

"Two weeks."

"Not a chance, Myles," Alan answered. "You're stuck with the cast whether you like it or not."

"Not."

"Perhaps your lonely sailing days are over."

Henry didn't have a chance to answer, because a tall, ebony-haired woman stepped through the doorway and held out her hands. "Henry? Welcome."

"Lily," Henry said, reaching to wrap the beautiful woman in his arms.

An uncomfortable twinge of jealousy shot through Jess, and she quickly squelched the feeling.

Henry made the introductions. The woman turned her warm violet gaze on Jess and smiled a welcome. "How wonderful to meet you," Lily said, offering a slim, white hand.

Jess began to feel more comfortable. "Thank you for offering to have us stay with you."

Lily smiled. "Henry gave us a wonderful three days in Seattle several years ago. I'm grateful to have the chance to return his hospitality. Please." She gestured gracefully toward the door. "Come in. You must be tired."

"This is our United Nations family," Alan said, as children of various sizes and races galloped down the large staircase centered in the foyer. "I'll tell you their names if they'll hold still for a minute."

The kids surrounded Jeremy and Sue and Alan attempted to introduce everyone. Before he could finish they ran through the house toward the backyard.

"Don't worry. There's nothing that can hurt them out there," Alan said.

"How many children were there?" Jess asked weakly.

"Seven," Lily answered, pride in her voice. "The youngest is five, the oldest eleven. We've adopted six of them, with one waiting for the paperwork to be completed."

"Are you sure you have room for us? I told Henry it would be easier if we stayed in a motel."

Lily laughed. "You haven't seen the rest of this crazy house yet. It's ridiculously big. And the children refuse to sleep alone, so there are plenty of extra bedrooms. Besides, we've been asking Henry to visit for years, but he's always too busy."

Jess followed Lily through the house, interested in Lily's description of the house's colorful history. Henry stayed close to her, occasionally touching her back or smiling down at her as if he was thrilled to have her with him.

Later, as the four adults enjoyed a quiet dinner, the conversation revolved around Jess and Henry's travels, with Henry describing how the heat wave in Montana had affected him.

"I can't believe you're taking a vacation." Alan opened a second bottle of wine and refilled the glasses.

"It's not like you to leave the business, Henry. You must be growing wiser in your old age."

Vacation? This was news to Jess. She sipped her wine and waited for Henry to answer. And what was this about business? Henry had said only last week that he was between jobs. He probably didn't want his friends to know he was out of work, she decided, even though he didn't act like someone who was very worried about his future.

Henry chuckled. "G.H. forced me into it."

Jess pretended interest in the portion of scallop casserole on her plate. The delicious new flavor couldn't compete with the conversation, though.

Lily leaned forward in her chair. "How is he doing?"

"Same as ever. I just talked to him on the phone a few minutes ago, and he sounded fine. I forget how old he is unless he reminds me."

Alan shook his head. "Is he still sneaking off to Las Vegas to gamble?"

"No, he's into fishing instead. That's how he met Jess." He smiled at her across the table. "Jess worked in Idaho, where G.H. likes to fish for Dolly Varden."

"For who?"

Jess laughed. "That's a kind of trout."

"Tell us about Seattle, Henry," Lily said. "Are you still building marinas?"

"Marinas?" Jess echoed.

Lily shot her a surprised look before turning her attention back to Henry. Her expression revealed her thoughts: why doesn't your friend know what you do for a living?

The proverbial stuff was hitting the fan, Henry concluded, looking over at Jess. He'd have to act as if it was no big deal and hope that worked. "Part of the family business, Jess. Years ago I began developing the family's waterfront property. We've been cleaning up some pretty rough areas."

"And the spices?" she asked.

"G.H.'s realm, since my father died suddenly last year. My brother, Peter, has a boat-building business."

"I'm sorry, Henry," Alan interjected. "We didn't get to see your father when we were in Seattle. I think he was out of the country at the time."

Lily nodded. "I lost my father two years ago," she said softly. "It's not easy."

Alan picked up his wineglass. "Let's drink to the future—and continued good health and friendship." His warm smile included Jess.

She tapped her glass against Henry's, avoiding his gaze as she drank the dry wine, and vowing to get some answers out of the man.

JESS COULDN'T SLEEP. Instead, she curled up on the padded window seat and turned her back to the dark yard below, admiring the private bedroom Lily had tactfully given her. A tiny blue-and-white-print paper decorated the walls, and a fluffy white comforter had covered the four-poster bed until Jess had turned down the sheets. White eyelet curtains fell in swirls to the polished oak floor. Martha Washington would have felt right at home, Jess decided, except for the electric lamp on the pine table.

There was a soft knock on the door, which came as no surprise. Henry and Alan had still been catching up with each other's lives when she and Lily had said good-night.

"Come in," Jess called quietly.

The door opened, and Henry peered around the corner. "Hi," he said.

"Come on in," she repeated.

He shut the door behind him. "I won't stay if you don't want me to, but I thought I'd say good-night."

Jess remained curled up on the window seat. "Henry, do I know you at all?"

His expression grew thoughtful as he sat beside her and put his arm around her shoulders. "You know the important things," he said, stroking her hair.

"Like what? That you have a broken arm? That your grandfather is G.H. Myles, a rich old man who likes to fish?"

"No," Henry said, looking down into Jess's eyes. "The important things, such as that I've fallen in love with you."

Jess's heart skipped a beat. "You've never said so."

"I didn't grow up in a family that made speeches." His tone was almost apologetic.

"Saying 'I love you' isn't a speech."

"I know." Henry smiled. "Unless you're a Myles."

"Oh." She'd give a million dollars to know what to say to him, but her mind remained blank.

"There's more."

"There is?" The man she loved had just said he loved her, and there was *more*? Was he going to stay in Pennsylvania? Was he an ax murderer? Did he have six wives and fifty children scattered across the Northwest?

"G.H. conned me into going on this trip. He was worried about your traveling alone and thought you needed someone to go with you."

"I *had* advertised for a passenger, but the responses were a little...weird."

"G.H. told me you were a friend of his, but I didn't believe him," Henry said cautiously.

Jess was becoming confused. "What do you mean?" she asked.

"My grandfather has a weakness for the ladies, and

the last one cost the family thousands of dollars to pay off. I confess—" he smiled down into Jess's puzzled eyes "—I thought you were another one after the old man's money."

Jess guffawed. "You're kidding."

He shook his head. "No, sweetheart. I'm not. I thought I had to be with you in order to keep G.H. from giving you money."

"That's why you were so cranky?"

"Cranky?" He lifted one eyebrow. "That's putting it mildly. There were other reasons."

Mistaken for a fortune hunter after an old fisherman's money—it was so ridiculous Jess found it vastly amusing. "What other reasons?"

"My broken arm, your hot car...and I hadn't expected two children, either."

"You survived," she countered dryly.

"Thrived," he corrected, caressing Jess's cheek. "You're not angry?"

"No." She wriggled into the comfort of his arms. "I've never been called a fortune hunter before. Makes me sound pretty mysterious and wicked."

"When I first saw you, I didn't blame G.H. for being protective."

"I don't believe that for a second, Henry. With my red nose and puffy eyes and all those tears? No way."

"Your legs," Henry insisted. "When I saw those legs I weakened."

"You want to see the legs again?" Jess asked in her Mae West imitation.

Henry feigned surprise. "Are you trying to seduce me here in this Colonial mansion with all its ghosts listening?"

"Yeah." Jess giggled. "Let's make history."

"Bad joke, good idea." He stood up and slung her

over his shoulder. "I can't carry you in my arms, but this way works well, too."

He dumped her on top of the four-poster bed.

"I hope this thing is sturdy," Jess said, reaching for Henry's waist.

"You *are* talking about the bed?"

She pretended to hesitate. "Of course."

He laughed softly and, with Jess's help, removed his clothes. She then pulled off her own shirt and let it drop to the floor.

Henry's kisses were urgent and needy; the feel of his bare skin against hers was electrifying. When he entered her, Jess matched him stroke for stroke, building slowly to a shattering climax. Even then, Henry didn't leave her. Hot and heavy, he stayed inside until, with deliberate motions, he reignited the passion once again.

Later, Jess wished she could have held him inside her all night long. Tomorrow, they would be in New York. And though he'd said he loved her, he hadn't said anything about staying with her.

"ALAN AND LILY want us to stay another day," Henry said at breakfast. "They'd like to show us some of the local history."

Jess put down her coffee cup. "I don't know, Henry. We should get going." She was glad they were alone for a few minutes. Alan had taken the children outside to hunt frogs in the pond, and Lily had excused herself to take a phone call.

"The kids would get to experience some history they might never have the chance to see again."

He sure knew her weak spot, Jess decided. "I know, but—"

"You'd get a day of rest from driving," he continued. "You can't tell me you don't need it."

"We haven't exactly been burning up the miles," Jess countered dryly.

"Still, sweetheart, you've been behind the wheel of that car every day." Henry smiled across the table, melting her objections. "You must be tired."

I'm scared, she wanted to tell him. But she stayed silent. She'd have liked nothing better than to stay in Pennsylvania for the rest of the summer and avoid her future for as long as she could. New York was only one state away, and Jess knew she had to prepare herself for being alone again. Henry didn't know that, though, and Jess tried to sound determined. "I need to get on with my life, Henry."

"Then use the phone here and make some calls," he said, unperturbed. "Maybe that will make you feel better."

Jess thought it over. "That's not a bad idea."

"See? I'm smarter than I look."

"This is true." She studied his laughing expression. The man certainly looked as if he were enjoying his vacation. "All right, you can have your extra day. But we leave on Wednesday. I promised the kids they could see dinosaur bones."

"Where?" He leaned back in his chair.

"At the Museum of Natural History."

"Oh, Lord," he sighed. "We're driving into New York City?"

"Sure." Jess pushed her plate away and leaned her elbows on the table. *Tell me where you're going next*, she wanted to plead. *Tell me you're not going home to Seattle now.*

She wondered how he would get home, whether his fear of airplanes was a lie, too. And did he really become claustrophobic on trains? How much had she believed that wasn't true? She kept her gaze on his face. "Isn't that where you wanted to go?"

Henry avoided her eyes and remained silent. It was a long five seconds. "Okay," he said, standing up to leave the table. "Dinosaur bones it is."

LATER THAT AFTERNOON, Jess sat on her bed making neat piles of money—twenties, tens, fives and ones. There were fewer twenties and more ones than she would have liked, but it was enough. It would have to be.

She'd have the bank in Idaho wire her her savings when she settled somewhere, and that money would keep her going throughout the next months. She planned to have a talk with Henry about the cost of the rooms—she didn't think he'd been telling the truth about that, either, and she didn't want to owe him a dime. She didn't want to have to feel grateful for the rest of her life to either G.H. or his grandson.

Henry was busy enjoying himself, touring the countryside, buying souvenirs and eating scrapple, the special sausage Lily's housekeeper had served them that morning. For him and his friends this was a summer vacation, not the move of a lifetime. That discrepancy only highlighted the differences between them; he was on holiday, and she was trying to survive.

One more day. It would be hard to sleep alone, to let go of the wonderfully intense physical relationship she and Henry shared. She'd miss his friendship, too. And, Jess concluded sadly, picking up the neat piles of money, she'd miss his love.

DAMPNESS HUNG in the morning air as the McCabes gathered to say goodbye to their guests. No one wanted to get into the car.

"Have a great time seeing the dinosaurs," Lily said, hugging Jess. "Come back again, anytime."

"Thanks for everything," Jess replied. "We'll have wonderful memories of Pennsylvania."

Henry and Alan exchanged quiet words as Henry stood against the open car door. He gave Lily another quick hug before getting into the car. Soon they were on their way, driving along a winding road that would meet the highway to New York.

Jess wanted to plead with the silent man next to her to say something. She needed to hear what his plans were, and if he was leaving her today. He seemed cheerful, but didn't have anything to offer in the way of conversation.

The children, tired after two days of constant activity, contented themselves with listening to music and coloring. Jeremy's ear wasn't bothering him, although he remained on medication. Earlier in the morning, Sue had begged to move to Pennsylvania so she could go to the same school as her new girlfriends. Jess empathized with her little daughter. There was a lot to be said for having girlfriends.

They stopped for a late breakfast, but Jess only picked at her food and drank too much coffee.

"You're not hungry?" Henry asked after polishing off a three-egg omelet with all the extras, and six slices of toast.

She shook her head. "Not really." She rested her chin in her hand and looked across the table at him. He looked healthier now than when she'd first seen him. More relaxed. Happier, too. She'd been good for him, Jess decided. And he'd been good for her. But it was time to call it a day. She took a deep breath, ready to let this be the last table they would ever share.

"Can I have your toast?" he asked.

Jess pushed her plate over to him.

"Thanks." He began to cover the slices with jelly. "Think you'll ever get used to Eastern accents?"

"By this time next year I'll probably have one of my own."

He laughed. "I doubt it."

"Where—" She wanted to ask where he'd like her to drop him off, but the words stuck in her throat. Jess took a swallow of coffee and tried again. "Where—"

"Where what?" Henry looked at her over the rim of his coffee cup. His gaze was warm and full of affection...and something else. He'd said he loved her. Once.

Get on with your life, she ordered herself. A couple of weeks in a car with a man didn't have to add up to heartbreak when the ride was over. Two separate people, that was what they were. Two people who'd enjoyed a wonderful friendship and an incredible sexual experience across half the United States.

"Where what?" he repeated.

"Where's that waitress?" Jess picked up her empty cup. "I could sure use some more coffee."

"You've had seven cups already." Henry shot her a worried look. "Are you feeling okay?"

"Sure," she replied airily. "Just looking forward to dinosaurs."

"Me, too," Jeremy added. "Have I ever seen any before?"

"No," Jess told him, glad of the diversion. "These are just the bones, you know."

The boy sighed. "I know that, Mom."

"Just checking," she said, watching the children color their place mats for the restaurant's coloring contest. "I can't wait to see them."

"Yeah, Mom," Sue said, not looking up. "We know."

The waitress refilled Jess's coffee cup, and Jess eyed the dark liquid warily. At this rate, she wouldn't sleep for the next three days.

HENRY FIGURED that Jess must have nerves of steel to drive in the city. She couldn't be used to bumper-to-bumper traffic like this, especially since she'd grown up in the Northwest. He didn't envy her the job of negotiating four lanes jammed with cars.

The hard part for him lay in deciding what to do next. Two weeks wasn't enough time to make a lifetime commitment. He'd always thought you were supposed to take it slowly, decide if you were compatible, spend lots of time together and give each other time to change your minds.

That was the part that had kept him a bachelor; somehow he always seemed to change his mind. There never seemed to be a good enough reason to work on the relationship. Women left his life as easily as they'd entered, frustrated because they couldn't get more emotion out of him, or tired of the workaholic habits that governed his life, or relieved to go on to someone who was more fun…or all of the above.

He's never had any regrets when a woman shut the door, so what on earth was wrong with him now? Henry shifted uneasily on the seat of the car and looked over at Jess. Her thick hair was piled on top of her head, her white T-shirt and rumpled denim skirt showed off her tan. But she looked worried.

He called himself an idiot. Of course she was worried—she had a few things on her mind. Henry silently berated himself as they drew closer to the city. Unable to voice words of commitment, he couldn't ask her to stay with him. Even though he'd told her he loved her, even though he meant the words.

He glanced guiltily at the glove compartment. Early this morning he'd checked the scribbled calculations on the money envelope, making sure he'd left a generous amount of cash inside to cover the past expenses.

He knew Jess would refuse to take his money if he handed it to her. At least they were even now.

But that didn't resolve the real issue. The real issue was how he could ask her to be part of his life. He worked all the time.

You don't have to work twenty hours a day.

How could there be room in his life for a wife and two—and maybe more—children?

Other men manage, even look happy about it.

Henry slumped against the seat. A G.H. Myles IV would be ridiculous.

The subject of his departure lay between him and Jess like something dark and dead on the front seat of the car, something that neither of them knew what to do with. Henry knew he was preparing to leave Jess and the children and go home to his comfortable lake-front town house, his marinas and a quick sail to the islands in September, if business permitted the time off.

The brakes squealed, catapulting him forward. He managed to catch himself before his bad arm slammed against the dashboard.

Jess swore loudly.

"What happened?"

"He cut me off," Jess muttered, pointing to the black Corvette racing away from them.

"I think that's just the way people drive around here," Henry said. He meant to be comforting, but she only glared at him.

"Oh? And you've been to New York before, I suppose?"

"Yes," he said, wisely choosing not to elaborate.

"Where's the map Lily gave us?"

Henry pulled a piece of paper out of his shirt pocket. "Here."

"Do you want to tell me where to turn before I have

a nervous breakdown and spend the rest of the summer sitting in the breakdown lane?"

"All that caffeine has made you cranky."

"I'm sorry."

He shrugged. "No problem." He quickly scanned the map and then read the passing green highway signs. "Go straight," he said, "but stay in the right lane because we'll be making a turn in about a mile."

"You'd think a big building like the Museum of Natural History would be easier to find," Jess muttered. She thought she'd get carsick from driving around in circles, as Henry successfully directed her past Central Park.

"It doesn't quite work that way," Henry replied. "But we should be getting close."

"I thought you'd been to New York before."

"Jumping into a taxi is different." He grinned at her. "It's more fun with you, though."

Jess didn't return the smile. She didn't dare take her eyes off the road for more than one second at a time. She gripped the steering wheel with sweaty hands. At least the traffic kept her from thinking too much about Henry's imminent departure. He'd said he loved her, but love and sex didn't automatically lead to a lifetime together. She was a grown woman—she knew that stuff.

By the time they passed the museum and made a U-turn on a street with a parking space, Jess wanted to crawl out onto the sidewalk and throw up. Maybe it was the oppressive heat, or the crowded city full of strangers.

Think of the future, she ordered herself. *Think of the real estate companies who want interviews.* She could make it with or without Henry Myles.

"What's wrong?" Henry asked, stepping onto the sidewalk.

Jess felt sticky. The city smelled. A pang of longing for a cool, mountain breeze stabbed through her. "I'm not sure I like New York."

"It grows on you. It's a pretty exciting place."

Jess looked over at the children. They stood on the sidewalk, identical suspicious expressions on their faces. *We're such hicks,* she thought. "I don't feel excited yet."

"Wait till you see the museum. It's not Fort Laramie," he said, teasing, "but it makes an attempt to educate."

Jess looked over toward the beautiful stone building. "You've been here before?"

He nodded. "You'll have a great time."

"So—" she took a deep breath "—are you going to go inside with us?"

"No."

It wasn't a surprise, Jess reminded herself. There was no reason to feel like dying. She kept what she hoped was a composed expression on her face as she looked up into his cool green eyes. "Then this is goodbye."

But Henry had seen the flash of pain. He made up his mind quickly, wondering for a split second why it had taken him so long to realize what he should have known all along. "No," he said. "I'll meet you back here at four-thirty."

Jess looked at her watch, hoping Henry wouldn't notice her trembling hand. "That's three hours from now."

"Not enough time?"

"Time?" she echoed.

Jeremy tugged on her arm. "There's a guy selling hot dogs."

"Just a minute, Jer." Jess tried to think but her brain didn't want to work.

"I'll meet you back here," Henry repeated. "All right?"

Jess nodded. "Then what?"

He knew she wasn't asking where they were going to eat supper. "Do you want to spend the night here in the city?"

"I don't think I do," Jess whispered. "I'm feeling a little overwhelmed." Understatement of the summer.

"Connecticut, then." He sounded pleased with the decision.

"You want to go to Connecticut with us?" Connecticut. What a great state, and she hadn't even seen it yet. The weight in her heart lifted.

"Sure." Henry smiled.

"I have the keys," Jess said, flustered. "You won't need them to lock the car. Just push the button down and hold it in."

He nodded. "No problem."

"Fine."

"I have some errands to do while I'm here in the city," Henry said.

"You don't have to explain." She could tell there was something going on, something he didn't want to tell her. She hesitated once more, but the children began to chase pigeons. Jess grabbed Sue's hand, wishing she were grabbing Henry instead. "See you later," she said.

He reached for her, placing a soft kiss on her lips before letting her go. "Right," he agreed, an unreadable expression in his green eyes. "See you later."

11

JESS GLANCED at her watch for what felt like the one-hundredth time. With all her heart she wished she could see Henry coming down the sidewalk. But he was late, *very* late, and she'd been too overwhelmed to ask where he was going. He had seemed to know his way around New York; maybe there were people he wanted to visit, or shops to see or restaurants to eat in. Damn it all to hell, she thought, where was Henry? And why had he needed to come to New York in the first place?

She paced back and forth on the sidewalk. She should have asked him what his plans were. She should have been more open, but since she'd felt him pulling away from her, she hadn't wanted to cling. She would never ask anybody for anything, especially not Henry.

She had her pride.

And the keys to the car.

And two children who thought eating hot dogs from a street vendor was about the greatest thing that had ever happened to them. Seeing as they were the most expensive hot dogs the children had ever eaten or would ever eat, Jess let them take their time.

She remembered the conversation from the other night. Maybe Henry had come all this way just to make sure his grandfather wasn't taken advantage of by a fortune hunter. That sounded ridiculous, and yet…

Jess thought of Henry's determination and pride. He probably would go to great lengths to protect his grandfather. But would he simply disappear when the job was done?

An hour later, Jess was still asking herself the same question. She couldn't wait any longer. It was time to move on. She was afraid the car would be towed away if she left it there any longer, and she didn't even want to contemplate what happened on the streets of New York when it grew dark. She'd seen the news on television and she didn't want to be here when darkness fell. She wanted to be safe in some nice little Connecticut motel.

"Come on, kids," Jess said.

"We're going back in the museum?" Jeremy asked hopefully.

Sue planted herself on the sidewalk and refused to budge. "Where's Henry?"

"We're going to find out, I hope," Jess answered. She led the children up the steps to the museum and inside, to the information desk. Perhaps Henry had called and left a message.

When Jess explained her problem, the woman looked at her as if she were out of her mind. Jess thanked her and took the kids outside.

"We'd better get Henry back right now," Sue demanded.

"Maybe he got lost."

"Thank you, Jeremy," Jess said.

"But he can get back," the child hurried to reassure his mother. "Henry knows maps, remember?"

Sue didn't look convinced.

Left with no choice, Jess returned her family to the station wagon. She and the kids could lock themselves in and wait. If a policeman instructed her to, she would move the car.

Half an hour seemed an eternity. Hot, humid air combined with smog to make Jess long for an open road. An open road anywhere, as long as Henry occupied the place next to her on the front seat. She didn't want to face the fact that Henry might not be joining them. Jess knew she should look in the back of the car to see if the crayon-coated duffel bag was still there, but she stalled. Five more minutes and she'd look.

"I have to go to the bathroom," Jeremy said from the back seat.

Sue piped up, "Me, too."

The bathroom trip took fifteen minutes, then Jess splurged and bought cold drinks. But when they returned to the car, there was still no sign of Henry.

"Wait here," she told the children. "Don't move away from the car for a second." She unlocked the car once again, climbed into the back seat and shoved aside the pile of sleeping bags and pillows. No duffel bag.

Jess surprised the kids by climbing over the back seat. She pushed the cooler to one side, swept a stack of coloring books toward the back window and looked behind her bags. There was Henry's unmistakable piece of luggage.

So where in the world was he? She didn't want to cry. She wanted to send out bloodhounds.

Harrigan cocked his head and "eeped" at her.

"Hello, baby," Jess said automatically.

"You're messin' up the car," Jeremy scolded. "Can we get in now?"

Jess climbed out of the car. "Sure. It's all yours."

Henry had left his clothes, but that wasn't much to leave behind, especially in a bag he'd end up throwing out as soon as he got home.

He was an hour and a half late. That was a pretty clear message in itself.

Jess forced herself to think about practical matters, such as gas, food and someplace to stay. She leaned across the seat and popped open the glove compartment. Her fingers closed around the plump envelope and she pulled it toward her. The neat figures—obviously Henry's writing—totaled her and Jeremy's scribbled numbers. He must have slipped money inside the envelope this morning, she realized, because she'd had it with her until last night. He'd planned to leave, and of course had been totally fair.

She called herself a total fool for not having believed what she'd seen coming. He hadn't wanted a messy goodbye scene and she hadn't wanted to see what was right under her nose—a man walking out of her life.

Making sure the children were settled in the car, she took one last look down the sidewalk. Of course, there was no reason to be worried about him, she realized. He'd be fine. His American Express card and gold Visa would get him safely home. He'd no doubt lied about his fear of flying, too, and was probably floating through the friendly skies right this minute. A vision of driving to the airport and pulling Henry off a plane flashed through Jess's mind, but it disappeared just as fast as it had arrived. She didn't have any idea how to get to the airport.

"C'mon, kids," she said. "Lock your doors and roll up the windows. I don't have any idea where we're going."

She was on her own, which was an amazing realization. She opened the map of the city and put it on the seat next to her, adjusted her sunglasses, turned on the radio and started the car. But she didn't pull immediately into the traffic. She continued to search the sidewalks to see if Henry was coming toward them. It was hopeless. The man was as gone as a man could get.

"What about Henry?" Sue asked.

"We can't leave him!" Jeremy added.

"I think Henry decided to go home," Jess said, careful to sound cheerful. She couldn't let the children know how disappointed she was. "He had some business in New York."

"Will he catch up with us?"

"I don't know."

"What's that supposed to mean?"

"It means," Jess said, tired and sticky and fighting tears. *"I don't know."*

"Oh."

"I'm sorry," Jess said. "Let's go to Connecticut, okay? Another new state."

HENRY WAS NOT HAVING a good time. The police station was crowded, dirty, noisy and totally oblivious to his problems. At least he'd bought Jess's ring before he was robbed of his wallet. This kind of thing happened to New Yorkers every day, over and over again, but never to Henry, and he was furious. He sat on a bench in the middle of the chaotic 24th Precinct police station, waiting to give his statement to someone in charge.

"Hey, you!"

Henry nodded to the policeman behind the desk.

"You the guy from the park?"

"Yes," Henry said, standing up. "Can I get out of here now?"

"You can tell your story to the officer over there." The man pointed to a slender, young black man wearing horn-rimmed glasses.

"About time," Henry muttered. He looked at his watch, then realized he didn't have it anymore. *Damn.* He could only hope that Jess would wait for him.

"Why don't you tell me what happened?" the officer said, after taking down Henry's name and address.

Henry took a deep breath, then began. "All I wanted to do was buy an engagement ring. I never thought I'd get lost or have my wallet stolen."

"The officer reported liquor on your breath, Mr., uh, Myles."

"Buying diamonds makes me nervous. I had a drink

at the Plaza afterward." That brief respite seemed like days ago instead of hours.

"The man you tackled pressed charges."

"I didn't hurt him."

"He says you did."

"How much damage could I do with a broken arm?"

"He's claiming it gave him a concussion."

"Don't expect me to feel sorry for him. He stole my wallet." Henry looked around until he saw the large wall clock. Five-thirty. He was already an hour late and time was running out. *Wait for me, Jess. Please.* "Is this going to take much longer?"

The young officer shrugged. "I suspect you've been the victim of a two-man pickpocket operation. I'll see what I can do."

After the police straightened out the situation, Henry stood on the sidewalk with seventy-nine cents in his pocket and Jess's ring tucked inside his sock. Flagging a taxi took longer than he'd anticipated, but he figured that was faster than walking.

"Museum of Natural History," he told the driver. *Be there, Jess. Please still be there.*

At least, Henry decided, he still had the ring. Hoping to appeal to Jess's romantic nature—the side of herself that she tried so hard to conceal from him and everybody else in the world—he'd taken a taxi downtown, straight to Fifth Avenue and Cartier. He'd wanted to present her with a hearts-and-flowers proposal. After all, this was to be his one and only proposal to a woman. A special woman.

He had planned to wait until they reached her precious Connecticut, and then ask her to marry him. He'd attempt to say all the right things, and then if he wasn't still nervous, he and she would discuss their future and he'd find out what she wanted out of life. He knew what he wanted: Jess. And the children. And maybe a couple more? If not, that was okay, too. He'd seen that movie with the three men who had to take care of a baby and hadn't found it all that funny. But on second thought, having a little Myles crawling around might be interesting. And he could teach the whole family how to sail. That is, if Jess consented to live in Seattle and trade her dreams of life on the east coast for a town house near Puget Sound.

The cabdriver interrupted Henry's daydreams. "Here you are, Mac."

Henry's heart sank. The station wagon wasn't where he'd left it. He looked through the cab's grimy windows, hoping to see the familiar "Famous Potatoes" Idaho license plate.

"Take me to the nearest Western Union," he said with a heavy sigh.

MARTHA ANSWERED the phone on the first ring.

"Of course I'll accept the charges, operator." There was a click, then his secretary's voice grew louder. "Henry, thank heaven, we've been praying you'd call."

"Martha, wire some money for me. A couple of thousand, anyway. And notify all the credit card companies, will you? I'm in New York, and my wallet's been stolen."

"Henry, listen to me. G.H. is in the hospital. He's had a stroke, and it doesn't look too good right now."

A cold chill stole over Henry's skin. Not G.H., too. Not right after his father. "How bad is it?"

"I don't know. No one does. Peter's at the hospital right now."

"Which one?"

She told him, giving the room number and doctor's name. "But I don't think you ought to call now, hon. Just get on a plane as soon as you can."

"You'll have to send money right away, Martha. I

owe a cabdriver a small fortune. And call in a reservation."

"Stay on the line," she said. "I'm going to make the calls and see what we need to do."

Henry waited for several long, tense minutes before hearing Martha's voice confirm the arrangements she'd made regarding money and transportation.

Twenty minutes later, he'd cashed the draft sent to him and returned to the waiting cab. Just in case Jess had come back, Henry instructed the driver to swing past the museum again before heading to Kennedy.

He knew he must face facts. It was as if Jess had vanished from the face of the earth, and he didn't know what in hell he was going to do about it. He couldn't recall the names of any Connecticut towns, much less the one where Jess had said she was going.

THE MOTEL ROOM seemed small and very empty at the same time. Jess paced. She just couldn't bear to sit still, worrying that maybe something had happened to Henry. Here she was, wearing a path in the carpet of this neat little overpriced motel room, and he could be lying hurt or dead on the streets of New York. Instead of trying to find him, she'd just driven away—okay, two hours later—as if it didn't matter.

But he *had* left the money.

She was thankful the children were quiet, tucked in their beds with the television on. Jess figured they were probably missing Henry as much as she was. She'd tried to cheer them by stopping for banana splits, but the conversation had revolved around Henry. Jeremy and Sue didn't understand why he'd left so abruptly, but were convinced he'd be coming back.

Jess knew she should try to explain that that wasn't going to happen, but she really didn't want to talk about Henry anymore. She knew if she opened her mouth she would either scream or cry.

She finally slumped at the foot of the bed. She would miss him. Boy, how she would miss him. New England loomed around her in a suddenly frightening way.

Here she'd thought she was so brave and independent.

Well, she was. And she'd summon up all those brave and independent qualities right after she went into the bathroom and cried for a couple of hours.

FIRST THINGS FIRST, Jess had decided. Getting a job was the most important thing. It had been a nervous Jess who left her children locked in a Connecticut motel room—watching heaven-knew-what-rated movies on cable television—to be interviewed for a real estate position in a busy coastal town just east of the New York border.

She hadn't felt comfortable, even though she was dressed in her one-and-only suit and wore matching beige earrings, panty hose and low white heels. It had been hell trying to iron the jacket and skirt on top of the dresser, with a folded bath towel as a pad, but she'd managed to look "dressed for success," instead of rumpled and sweaty. Still, it was a relief to be back in the cool motel and dressed in her favorite khaki shorts and T-shirt.

"Did you get the job?" Sue looked away from the television long enough to glance at her mother. "And can we go swimming now?"

"No, and yes," Jess said, gazing longingly at the telephone. Maybe she should call G.H. and find out if Henry was all right. No, she decided firmly, turning away. It was better to make a clean break. No whining phone calls from Jessica Whalen.

JESS KEPT DRIVING, and buying newspapers and being interviewed. And driving some more. The Connecticut towns seemed too ritzy, too Colonial chic for her mountain blood. She didn't feel at home yet.

Maybe she was asking too much, Jess pondered while sipping a diet cola at a fast food restaurant off Interstate 95. The place was enormous, part of a highway rest area with gift shops and a snack bar inside. The air-conditioning worked, too. Henry would have been pleased. She sighed, and picked up her hamburger.

Pretty soon she would have to dig her waitress uniform out of the back of the car and search for restaurant work. Help Wanted signs were everywhere; she'd never seen so many in her entire life. She felt certain they were minimum wage jobs, but still... Her money wouldn't last forever, and she and the children were ready to settle down.

She surveyed the classified ads once more, just in case she'd missed something the first time.

"Where are we, Mom?"

Jess smiled at Jeremy. It hurt to smile, she realized, because she wanted to scream and cry and curse Henry Myles for breaking her heart. Did kids know a fake smile when they saw one? "Almost at the end of Connecticut."

"Oh." He thought for a minute. "Then what?"

Good question. "How does Rhode Island sound to you?"

"Is it an island?"

"No, it's a state, the smallest one in the whole country, as a matter of fact," Jess said, pulling the map in front of her to look. "It's not very big, but it's on the ocean. We might as well get a view of what we've traveled all this way for. And I have a job interview in Warwick, a city there."

"Okay," Sue agreed. "Then we call Henry."

"Sue, sweetie, I don't know where Henry is. I promised to take him to New York and that's what I did." It sounded good when she put it that way.

"He didn't say goodbye."

Jess sighed. "I know, but that's not the point." But of course, she knew that was the point, exactly.

"I don't get it," Jeremy said.

Jess stood up and tossed the trash in the plastic bin. "That makes three of us."

"QUIT ACTING like I'm dying," the old man grumbled. "No need to look at me that way."

"You had a stroke," Henry said calmly. G.H. had been complaining for days, which was a definite sign of his returning good health. "We thought you were going to die."

"It would take more than a mild stroke to kill me."

"Obviously," Henry said.

"What's the matter with you? You're mopey. That arm of yours still botherin' you?"

Henry shook his head. "Not at all. I tried to talk Alan into taking the cast off in Pennsylvania, but he wouldn't." Thank goodness. He thought of the man with the concussion whose partner probably still had Henry's credit cards.

"Then what's the matter?" G.H. grumbled. "You look like you're ready to leap out of this room. Go back to the business. Somebody should be there to take care of things since they won't let me use the damn telephone."

"You're supposed to be recovering. You're not supposed to be using the phone."

"I'm just a little numb on one side of my body and they act like I'm dead."

"No one could think that, not from all the noise you make."

G.H. squinted toward his grandson. "You sent Peter home, didn't you?"

Henry nodded. "He needed the rest. But he'll be back next weekend."

"Hmm. You won't say a word about your vacation with my little friend. Why not?"

"Your little friend is quite a woman."

G.H. chuckled. "Shook you up, eh, boy?"

Henry thought of the ring sitting on top of the dresser in his very lonely bedroom. "Right to the core."

"Good, good." He frowned. "So what the hell are you doin' here? She come back with you?"

"I don't know where she is," Henry said, pain etching his voice.

"What the hell does that mean? You let that good woman get away? Thought you had more sense," he grumbled.

"I lost her."

"You *lost* her?"

"I was mugged in New York."

"Mugged?"

Henry shrugged. "Yeah, well…it's a long story."

"I don't have plans for this afternoon, do you?"

"Lord, you're a cantankerous old man." But Henry smiled down at his grandfather. At least G.H. was alive to give him a hard time. "I left Jess at a museum while I went to Cartier's—"

"You?" G.H. cackled. "In a jewelry store?"

"I thought I'd ask your friend to marry me."

The old man was shocked into silence. Henry went to the window and looked out over the city. It was almost sunny. "I got the ring, but lost the woman. Guess you could say it was not one of my better days."

"I'm probably the only Myles man who's had any luck with women. Generations of 'em seem to have a hell of a time hangin' onto any woman of any consequence."

"Which is why you wanted to help me out. You put me in a car with a woman and two children and a parakeet and a bowl of smelly hermit crabs and expected me to bring home a wife."

"Well," G.H. laughed delightedly. "I didn't know about the wildlife."

"Would it have made any difference?"

"No, and I didn't expect you to bring home a wife, either. I wanted you to have some fun."

Henry ignored that part. "By the time I made it back to the museum, Jess and the kids and the car were gone."

"What did you expect her to do? Drive around New York and hope she'd run into you?"

"No. I hoped she left a message." Henry turned away from the window and sat back down in the chair by G.H.'s bed. "I checked with the museum. Nothing. She just drove off." And she must have felt deserted, as if he had left her on purpose, as if he didn't want to say goodbye and just took off. He hated thinking about what she must be feeling. It kept him awake nights. "Do you remember if she said where she was going?"

G.H. frowned. "No, sorry, boy. She just talked about New England and eating lobster and walking near the ocean."

"There's a lot of Atlantic coast to cover."

"You've always been a determined man."

"True."

"You inherited that from me," G.H. stated happily. "Now get out of here."

IT WAS TRUE, Henry thought later, sitting alone in his office. Determination was inherited, a strength of the Myles family, which got them in trouble sometimes, if they were after the wrong thing. He picked up a new road atlas and opened it to the page Connecticut and Rhode Island shared. The names of hundreds of small towns looked back at him.

"Where are you, Jess? Where in the hell are you?"

HAPPY HOLLOW RESORT, of Pawcatuck, Connecticut, comprised eight small red cabins, only five feet apart. The cabins formed a line facing a grassy lawn that held rusted croquet wickets. A person who wasn't paying attention could trip and break an ankle, Jess figured, but so far no one had, at least not during the week that she and the children had lived there.

Hanging her wet laundry on the small clothesline between two scrub pine trees, Jess decided that *cozy* would be a kind word to describe her Happy Hollow cabin. She wanted to feel kind. But she didn't. She felt scared and alone. Her years as a single parent, however, had taught her to be resourceful and self-sufficient.

It had been ridiculously easy to find a job as a waitress in a colonial inn just two miles away. She'd also found Chrissie, a thirteen-year-old whose mother didn't allow her to work, but did approve of her baby-sitting. Chrissie's mother obviously didn't have any rules about jewelry, because the girl wore five earrings in one ear and three in the other. It was a phenomenon that impressed Sue no end. Even Jeremy had shown a passing interest and a grudging admiration for the courage required to have one's ears pierced eight times.

Jess spent all her spare time studying. Next week she would be taking the exam for her Rhode Island real estate license. Two different agencies wanted to talk to her after she passed, but until then she was content to earn money waiting tables. One of the real-estate agencies had offered her a typing job until she passed, but Jess couldn't type and wanted to learn her way around the area first.

Pawcatuck was a small area on the Rhode Island–Connecticut border. The town of Westerly, Rhode Island, was just minutes away, and the ocean stretched on from there. She'd driven along Route 1, and down the long roads to the beaches, trying to decide where she felt comfortable. She liked Wakefield, a busy little town minutes from the ocean. And she liked the small-town feeling of Charlestown, too. She could work in either place, if she passed the exam. But it all felt so strange that she was having doubts about what she'd done.

Despair set in after she called Gayle and learned the renters had moved to her house. Someone else living in her home didn't seem right. Not while she was living here in a Happy Hollow cabin.

The cross-country trip seemed like a long-ago dream. She'd had the photos processed, but couldn't bear to see them. Henry looked good, too good.

Hard work helped. Jess finished pinning her uniforms to the clothesline, and eyed the filthy station wagon with distaste. The time had come to attack the inside of the car and remove all traces of the long journey. Once she had collected all the trash she would hose down the Chevy at a car wash and vacuum the inside. She didn't even ask the children to help—her own private demons forced her to crawl around the car with a trash bag.

Finding Henry's expensive camera, still tucked under the seat, was an unexpected revelation to Jess. She had forgotten all about it, but she knew Henry would never have left it behind. Only amnesia would have made him forget his camera.

She hesitated for a moment before grabbing her jar full of loose change—tip money—from her dresser and walking next door to the pay phone at the grocery store. How many spice companies could there be in Seattle?

A call to Seattle information answered her question. Then she fed an enormous number of coins into the phone, and waited.

When a receptionist answered, Jess asked for Henry. Her heart in her throat, she was put on hold.

"Mr. Myles's office. May I help you?" The woman sounded cheerful, not at all as if her boss had died recently or was missing.

"Is this Henry Myles's office?"

"Yes, it is."

Jess took a deep breath. "Is he in?"

"He's in a meeting right now. Would you like to leave a message?"

A meeting. That meant he wasn't dead.

"Ma'am?" the woman prompted.

"Oh, okay." Jess thought quickly. "Tell him I made it to the Rhode Island border. To Pawcatuck."

"Who's calling?"

"He'll know. And tell him I have his camera."

"Is there a number where you can be reached?"

"There isn't one. But—"

"Is this *Jess*?"

"Yes, but—"

"Where *are* you?"

"Happy—"

She was interrupted by a recording. "Your three minutes are almost up. Please hang up or stay on the line for further charges after the party you are calling has disconnected."

"Hollow," Jess said, wondering if the secretary could hear her over the operator's voice. She hung up the phone, feeling ridiculous. She'd already done more than her pride would have normally allowed her to do. She'd let Henry know where she was.

So he was in a meeting—the bastard. Back in his own world. She wondered how the secretary had known her name, and what difference it made where she was. The man hated to fly, was claustrophobic on trains and couldn't drive. So how did he get back to Seattle? Magic carpet?

12

"WHERE'S THAT DAMN MAP?" Henry tossed neat piles of papers from his desk onto the floor with little concern for where they landed.

"It's—" Martha began, pointing to the couch.

"Never mind." Henry charged across the room and grabbed the atlas. "I've got it." He found the page he wanted and looked up at his secretary. "Tell me exactly what she said."

"She made it to the Rhode Island border, to some place called Paw-something."

"Paw-something?" he repeated. "That's *it*?"

Martha prayed for patience. She also added an extra prayer that Henry would find the woman called Jess and live happily ever after and that she, Martha Briggs, could resume normal secretarial duties and never have to listen to Henry's new Rolling Stones tape again. She had just grown accustomed to the jazz, and now he'd changed. "The telephone operator interrupted, Henry, but Jess said she was staying at a place called Happy—"

Henry's green eyes flashed. "Happy what?"

Martha sighed. "Happy *something*. I couldn't catch it all."

"Happy something," he repeated dismally. "Happy something in Paw something, on the Rhode Island border."

"That's right. She said to tell you she has your camera." The phone rang, and Martha reached across Henry's desk to pick up the receiver.

"I'm not taking any calls," Henry said, not looking up from the map. "Except from Jess, of course, and don't let anyone tie up my line."

"He's in a meeting," Martha said into the phone. "I'd be happy to take a message for you."

"At least Rhode Island can't have too much of a border. Most of it's on the ocean," Henry muttered, tracing the dark line with his index finger.

"I'm sorry, G.H., Henry can't be reached right now." There was a pause. "No, you didn't hear his voice in the background. That's the radio."

"Tell him I'll call back," Henry mouthed.

"I'll have him return your call as soon as possible." Martha hung up the phone and made a face. "I hate it when you make me lie to him."

Henry ignored her. "Pawtucket! How does that sound to you?"

"It could be," she said slowly. "Where is it?"

"The Rhode Island border," he stated triumphantly. "On the Massachusetts line. What do you think, Martha? Could this be the place?"

Martha smiled. "I think I'd better get on the phone and book you a flight to Rhode Island."

RHODE ISLAND'S Green Airport was jammed with summer travelers, but Henry managed to locate a bank of telephones near the check-in counters. After closing himself inside a booth, he leafed through the phone book looking for Happy places in Pawtucket.

He dialed every one he could find, but no one had a room occupied by Jess Whalen. When he'd exhausted motels, he started in on restaurants. Still no luck. Then he dialed every single real estate agency listed in Pawtucket. No one had heard of Jess.

Disgusted, hot and frustrated, Henry rented a car and purchased a large, detailed map of Rhode Island. He spread it across the hood of the sporty red Mazda and stared at it as if waiting for it to talk back. She'd said the Rhode Island border. Well, Jess? Massachusetts or Connecticut?

Bingo. Henry hopped in the car and sped toward the entrance ramp to Interstate 95 south. When he was certain he was on the right highway, he pulled a cassette tape from his shirt pocket and slid it into the car's tape deck. The gutsy rhythm of the Rolling Stones poured from the speakers, and Henry tried to memorize the lyrics as he raced along toward Pawcatuck, Connecticut and Jess.

"THERE'S A MAN asking for you out front."

Jess finished ladling thick, steaming chowder into serving bowls and turned around, only then realizing the hostess was talking to her. "Asking for me?"

Brenda nodded. "I put him at number 12."

Jess arranged the bowls of chowder on a large tray. Number 12 was a table for two in the corner. Whoever wanted her didn't have a view of the ocean. The way the fog was rolling in, though, no one dining at the Colonial Manor would see much of the Atlantic tonight.

She stepped through the swinging doors into the dimly lit dining room and headed for table 9. A busboy clearing nearby tables blocked her view of number 12. In the midst of filling extra requests from the large group of elderly tourists, Jess caught sight of the mysterious customer.

Green eyes met her gaze; his unsmiling mouth offered no clue to his feelings. Jess willed her knees to hold her up as she approached Henry's table.

"What in hell are you doing here?" She spoke in a low voice. Despite the restaurant's huge size, the owners prided themselves on the intimate atmosphere and kept noise to a minimum.

Henry tossed aside the heavy leather-bound menu. "Looking for you, Jess."

"You got my message."

He nodded.

"So," she murmured, hoping he wouldn't hear the pain in her voice, "you want your camera."

Surprise lit his eyes. "No. Throw it in the ocean, for all I care."

Jess held her pencil poised over the order pad. "Then you're here for dinner? How nice. What would you like? The special tonight is grilled mako shark, served with your choice of—"

"Jess, damn it! Listen to me, I don't—"

"Want the shark. I see." She pretended to think. "Then what about a nice steamed lobster?" She leaned toward Henry, the man who had deserted her in the middle of New York City. "You could soak your head in the melted butter."

"I just want to talk to you, Jess."

The words were spoken through gritted teeth, Jess noticed with satisfaction. Good. She wanted to make him angry, to make him feel as bad as she'd felt when she realized he had left her. The sneaky coward. "You sneaky coward," she said.

"All *right,*" he snapped. "I didn't come all this way to eat lobster, but just give me anything."

"Anything," she repeated. "Excellent, sir." She spun around toward the kitchen and, after checking to see how her other tables were doing, almost ran through the swinging doors. The anger felt wonderful—if she could only stay in that state until he left, she wouldn't disgrace herself by crying. She scribbled an order for the kitchen. By the time she was ready to serve Henry his first course, he'd had the cocktail waitress bring him a beer.

"Here you are, sir."

"Jess, we need to—" He stared at the plate in front of him. The ring of clam shells looked suspiciously as if they had just been dug out of the sand and pried open, and a small container of hot sauce sat in the middle of the plate. "What are they?"

"Littlenecks on the half shell. A Rhode Island delicacy."

"Clams?"

Jess shook her head. "Quahogs. I think you're supposed to swallow them whole."

"You're trying to make me sick," Henry said.

"I'm trying to make you leave."

"No way, sweetheart." Henry resisted the urge to grip her wrist. He suspected that would only make her angrier. "You need to give me a chance to explain."

Out of the corner of her eye, Jess saw her table of four wave to her. Dessert time. "Sorry, Mr. Myles. I'm working right now." She hurried away, ready to recite the dessert menu for the twenty-eighth time tonight.

"I WAS MUGGED," he said, when Jess put the red lobster in front of him.

"Here's the bib," she said, handing him the plastic covering that came with the lobster dinner. "Prying them apart can be pretty messy."

"Did you hear me, Jess?" Henry ignored his dinner. "I said I was mugged."

"Where?"

"In Central Park." This time he reached to grab her hand. "Which is why I couldn't meet you at the museum."

Jess stared down at him and saw only honesty in his eyes. The large weight on her heart eased slightly, and she felt as if she could breathe without pain again. "Really?"

He nodded. "Really."

"Waitress!" A man from the neighboring table beckoned. "Could we have some more decaf here, please?"

Jess nodded. "Of course." She turned back to Henry. "It's getting late. You should be my last customer."

"I'll work my way through this lobster and wait for you outside."

The determined look on his face made Jess want to smile for the first time in ten days. "It's going to take another hour or so."

"I can wait," Henry said.

And he did. When Jess finally stepped out into the fog, Henry materialized to take her arm.

"Over here," he said. "Notice anything?"

"No cast," Jess observed. "Congratulations."

"I drove myself from the airport," he stated proudly. "Felt as if I'd been set free."

"Let me see." Jess peered at the bandaged arm. "How does it feel?"

"Fine," he said, wrapping her in his embrace. "Especially now."

Jess took a step back, determined not to give in to passion. There were a few things to be settled between herself and Henry Myles, and kissing him wouldn't give her any answers. "Tell me about the mugging."

Henry sighed, and gestured toward the parking lot. "Come on, I'll follow you home." He stopped and looked around the nearby empty parking area. "Where's the wagon?"

"It's in need of major repairs, so I got a ride with one of the busboys."

"Come on, then." He unlocked the passenger door and tucked her into his car.

"This is a switch," she said, as Henry climbed behind the wheel and, following Jess's directions, steered the car along the winding road.

"I like it." He smiled over at her. "How are the kids? I've missed them."

"They miss you, too, but they're okay. They like the beach, after they got used to the saltwater."

Henry reached over and took her hand. "Jess—"

"The mugging," Jess interrupted. "You promised to

ell me about it." She wanted to believe him, but nagging doubts edged her thoughts. And yet, looking over it his strong profile, Jess knew she loved him. Whether hat was a good idea or not, she wasn't certain.

"All right," he said, but remained silent until they drove into Happy Hollow. He parked the car in the clearing in front of cabin 8 and shut off the engine. 'Can we talk here?"

Jess looked toward the lighted windows and decided that Chrissie would wait a few more minutes before going home. The kids would have been asleep for hours. She shifted in her seat, curling up to face Henry. 'Okay."

He took a deep breath, telling her the entire story of his experience in New York, leaving out only the part about buying an engagement ring.

"Poor G.H. How is he doing now?"

"Recovering quite well. The doctors have finally allowed him to have a phone in his room, so he calls me every hour to make sure the company still exists."

"I'm glad you're both all right."

"I'm a lot better now that I know where you are." He took her hand, playing gently with her fingers. "Have you had your walks by the ocean, Jess?"

She nodded in the darkness. "It's very beautiful."

"Do you like it here?"

"I'm getting used to it." She hesitated, then admitted, "I didn't think it would be this different, or that I would miss the mountains so much."

"Come back to Seattle with me, Jess."

"Henry—"

"I mean it, sweetheart. You don't belong here. Haven't you realized this whole idea of yours was crazy to begin with?"

Jess stiffened. "It's not crazy to want a better life for your family."

Henry continued, unaware that he'd insulted her.

"What's better about this? You're still waitressing, Jess."

"Just until I pass my real estate exam next week."

"I'll give you any job you want with the company, if that will make you happy. Come back with me, Jess. Marry me. You and the children will never want for anything."

Silence filled the car.

"I love you, Jess."

"I love you, too," she answered softly. Grabbing the handle of the door, she tugged it open. "That's not the point."

"Then what is?"

She turned around to meet his confused gaze before climbing out of the car. "I'm not going backward. And I don't need to be rescued by you, or anybody. I'm perfectly capable of surviving without your damn job." Tears made her words sound ragged, but she didn't care. She slammed the door and hurried inside to the cabin, leaning against the refrigerator until she heard Henry's car drive away.

After paying Chrissie, Jess checked on the sleeping children, who shared the double bed in the one and only bedroom, then opened the pull-out sofa. *What's the point, Jess?*

The question kept her awake long after she'd showered and shampooed the food odors from her hair. Did she want to be alone for the rest of her life because she couldn't admit loving Henry—and being loved by him—made her happy?

The rest of her life. Ominous-sounding words, Jess decided, tossing and turning on the meager mattress. For months she'd done nothing but make decisions. Decisions that would affect the rest of her life, and the children's, too. And now Henry's. But she wasn't going to marry him simply because she couldn't survive otherwise. No matter how much she loved him.

Fool. You're not giving up anything to marry that man, nothing that matters anyway. Just a carful of pride and a lifetime of loneliness.

Jess buried her face in her pillow and refused to cry. How could she feel sorry for herself when she acted like such a jerk?

THE SOUND OF A CAR DOOR slamming woke Jess from a miserable dream. Harrigan had died and her car, a purple hearse, had been filled with squawking parakeets of all colors. "Jerk," they screamed at her.

She sat up, blinking in the murky green light. Harrigan chattered in his cage under the blanket, and Jess climbed out of bed and lifted off the cover to make sure he was all right.

"Hello, baby," she crooned.

"Eep." He flapped his wings.

"Glad you're alive." Jess looked past the bird cage to the window, where she saw a red Mazda parked less than ten feet away. Henry, sitting cross-legged on the hood, waved when he saw her.

"Sometimes you get a second chance, Harrigan," Jess said, already hurrying outside. Her bare feet almost skimmed across the dewy grass as she raced to the car.

Henry lifted a cup of coffee from a paper bag. He held it out to her. "Care to join me?"

Jess climbed up on the hood and sat beside him. Taking the coffee, she cradled it in her hands.

"Breakfast?" He shoved a box of doughnuts toward her.

She selected a cinnamon-coated one. "Thanks." She bit into the soft cake, deciding it was the best thing she'd tasted in almost two weeks. "What are you doing here, Henry?"

"Waiting for sunrise."

Jess sipped the hot coffee. "I don't know how to tell you this, but we're facing west."

He shrugged. "I don't have much sense of direction."

She took a deep breath and spoke from her heart. "I think facing west is a pretty good idea."

After long, silent minutes, she looked over at him. Henry wore the same clothes he'd had on last night, but now they looked rumpled, as if he'd slept in them. A day-old beard stubbled his serious face. "I'd like to think you mean that."

"I do."

His mouth softened into a smile. "Come here," he said, removing the cup from her hand and pulling her against him. He kissed the sugar off the corner of her mouth before wrapping her in his arms. "I blew it last night. I wanted to sweep you off your feet with a romantic proposal—I even bought the diamond ring in New York—and then I ended up saying all the wrong things."

"I said the wrong things, too," Jess murmured against his neck. The doughnut fell unnoticed onto the hood of the car.

"Let's try it again."

She nodded. "Okay."

He cleared his throat. "Marry me, Jess. I don't want to live without you and I'll love you until the day I die. I'll be a good father, too. I promise." He pulled away so he could look down into her face. He winced when he saw her smile. "Too corny?"

Jess shook her head. "Just right, Henry Myles. I love you with all my heart."

His lips claimed hers for a long moment, until Henry reluctantly pulled away. "Come on," he said. "I'll help you pack."

"Now?"

"Yeah." He grinned at her. "I'm anxious to take you all home."

Jess's heart sank at the thought of another long trip across the country. "I'll need to get the car fixed."

"Sell it," Henry said, fishing the ring out of his pocket and reaching for Jess's hand. "We're going to fly."

"I thought you were afraid to fly."

"I lied," he murmured as he slid the ring onto her finger.

Jess stared at the diamond sparkling on her hand. Could something so beautiful be real? Her voice grew weak. "And trains?"

Henry sighed. "I lied about the claustrophia, too."

Jess pulled back from his embrace and smiled up into his handsome, familiar face. "What else did you lie about, Henry?"

"Not about loving you, Jess." He leaned closer, brushing his lips against hers in a tantalizing motion. "Never about that."

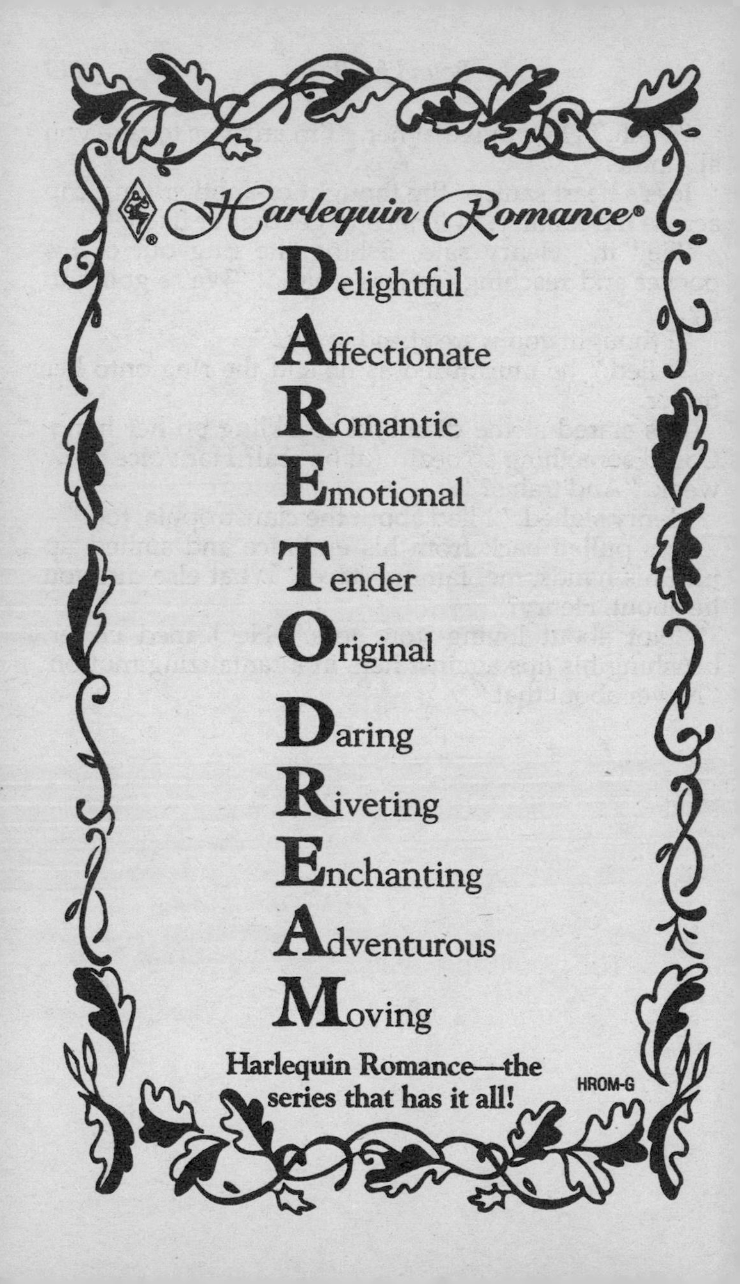
Harlequin Romance®
Delightful
Affectionate
Romantic
Emotional
Tender
Original
Daring
Riveting
Enchanting
Adventurous
Moving
Harlequin Romance—the series that has it all!
HROM-G

HARLEQUIN PRESENTS
men you won't be able to resist
falling in love with...

HARLEQUIN PRESENTS
women who have feelings
just like your own...

HARLEQUIN PRESENTS
powerful passion in
exotic international settings...

HARLEQUIN PRESENTS
intense, dramatic stories that will keep you
turning to the very last page...

HARLEQUIN PRESENTS
The world's bestselling romance series!

PRES-G

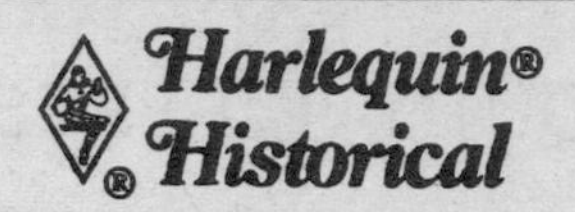

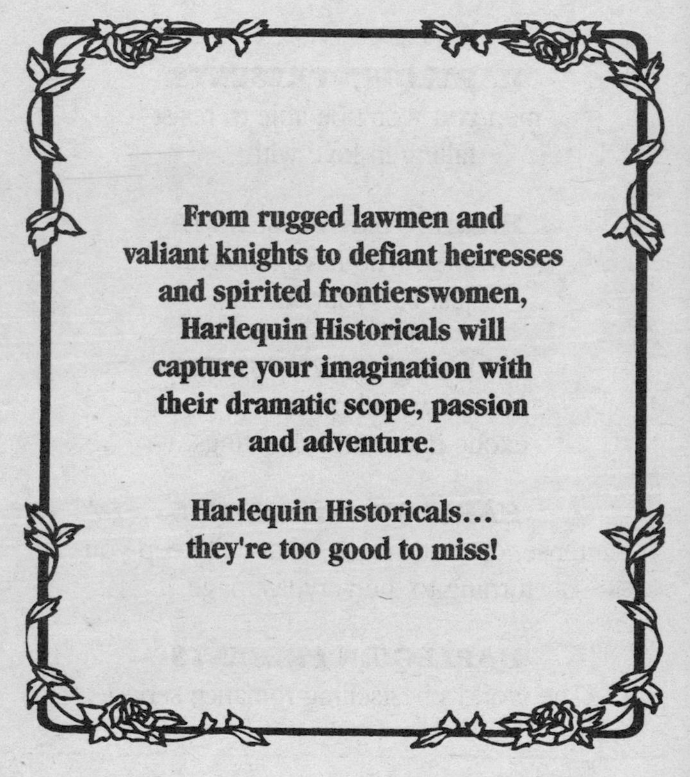

From rugged lawmen and
valiant knights to defiant heiresses
and spirited frontierswomen,
Harlequin Historicals will
capture your imagination with
their dramatic scope, passion
and adventure.

Harlequin Historicals...
they're too good to miss!

HHGENR

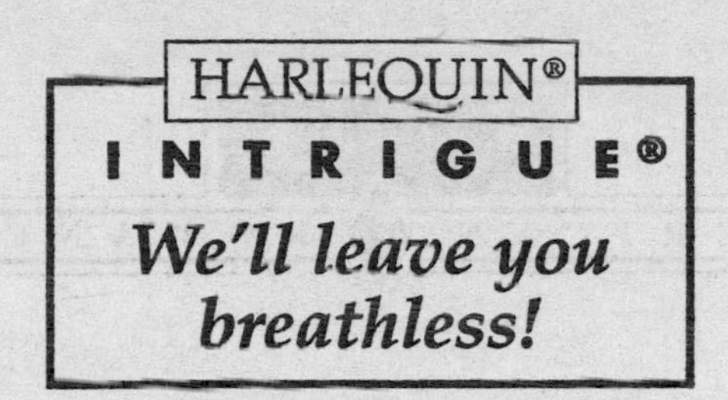

If you've been looking for thrilling tales of contemporary passion and sensuous love stories with taut, edge-of-the-seat suspense— then you'll *love* **Harlequin Intrigue**!

Every month, you'll meet four new heroes who are guaranteed to make your spine tingle and your pulse pound. With them you'll enter into the exciting world of Harlequin Intrigue— where your life is on the line and so is your heart!

THAT'S INTRIGUE—DYNAMIC ROMANCE AT ITS BEST!

HARLEQUIN®

INTRIGUE®

INT-GENR

LOOK FOR OUR FOUR FABULOUS MEN!

Each month some of today's bestselling authors bring four new fabulous men to Harlequin American Romance. Whether they're rebel ranchers, millionaire power brokers or sexy single dads, they're all gallant princes—and they're all ready to sweep you into lighthearted fantasies and contemporary fairy tales where anything is possible and where all your dreams come true!

You don't even have to make a wish...
Harlequin American Romance will grant your every desire!

Look for Harlequin American Romance
wherever Harlequin books are sold!

HAR-GEN